WWI
THE NAKED SOLDIER

First published 2022

Copyright © Gerry Mills 2022

The right of Gerry Mills to be identified as the author of this work has been asserted in accordance with the Copyright, Designs & Patents Act 1988.

All rights reserved. No part of this book may be reproduced, stored in a retrieval system, or transmitted in any form or by any means, electronic, electrostatic, magnetic tape, mechanical, photocopying, recording or otherwise, without the written permission of the copyright holder.

Published under licence by Brown Dog Books and
The Self-Publishing Partnership Ltd, 10b Greenway Farm, Bath Rd, Wick, nr. Bath BS30 5RL

www.selfpublishingpartnership.co.uk

ISBN printed book: 978-1-83952-478-3
ISBN e-book: 978-1-83952-479-0

Cover design by Andrew Prescott
Internal design by Andrew Easton

Printed and bound in the UK

This book is printed on FSC certified paper

WWI
THE NAKED SOLDIER

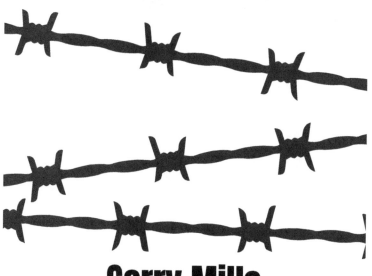

Gerry Mills

BROWN DOG BOOKS

PREFACE

The war.

The war to end all wars.

This was the war that started in the summer of 1914 and would be 'all over by Christmas.'

The war that will be known as 'The Great War'.

Later to be named 'World War One' after the devastation of World War Two.

The war that caused the deaths of 10 million combatants and 7 million civilians with 20 million casualties resulting in 20% of the world's population being affected by this carnage.

The war that left hundreds of thousands of families destitute, with no one to provide for them, living in poverty while the warlords and upper echelons of society lived it up in the Roaring Twenties. Towns and cities were destroyed and people were left homeless, struggling to pick up where they had left off before the war.

The war that left very few unaffected, with most people suffering loss either directly or through family and friendship channels.

The war that, had it not happened, would see 1 billion more people on the planet today (2022), equal to another 12% of the current population of 7.8 billion.

Without WW1 and the harsh penalties put on the defeated, it could even be assumed WW2 would not have happened – a very big assumption.

And what caused this carnage?

Queen Victoria had something to answer for. She had three wayward and simple-minded grandsons, George, Wilhelm and Nicholas, who, over the latter part of the 1800s and the first decade of the 1900s, were determined to outdo each other in military force, conquering countries in the Far East, Africa, South America and any other country they could steal the natural resources from. But not all blame lies with the old lady or her German husband or her German-speaking children for whom English was a second language. But who does carry the blame if not Queen Victoria?

Prior to 1914, various nations had formed alliances in order to protect one another from the imperialistic ideals of the most powerful countries. The German Navy had been developed to compete with their British counterparts with George and Willy ready for action with Nicky watching with interest. So, the scene became set for confrontation. It all came to a head on 28th June 1914 with an assassination in one of the hotchpotch of 'countries' that had been gathered together under the Austria-Hungarian Empire. Too many differences of culture, language and religion to be classed as an empire. Too many diverse nationalities to form a cohesive stand against the might of Britain, Germany and Russia. The scene was set for an event to trigger a domino effect within the grand and the small nations.

And it did.

Gavrilo Princip, a nineteen-year-old, deranged Serb nationalist sympathiser, found himself in a back street in Sarajevo with a horse and carriage coming towards him containing some little-known Austrian royal and his devoted wife. The man, a student, had a loaded pistol in his hand. A planned attack, by six young idealists, to murder the couple had recently failed. The carriage with the royals inside had got separated from the rest of their procession due to the driver heading in the wrong direction. While the driver stopped to correct his route, Princip, who was at the location, jumped on the running board of the car and shot both the occupants at point blank, killing then with a bullet each.

So, the son of the boss of the crumbling Austria-Hungarian Empire and his wife were no more and it did not take long for the repercussions to start.

Austria blamed Serbia and demanded concessions from the Serbs, the majority of which the Serbs agreed to, but it was not enough and Austria eventually declared war, something they did with the backing of Germany. Serbia, however, had an ally in Russia and, as Austria declared war on Serbia, both Austria and Germany found themselves at war with the Russians. Russia had an ally in France, resulting that France and Germany were to be at war with each other (again). To further complicate the situation Britain had guaranteed the Belgians' neutrality in the event of a threat to its sovereignty and independence. When Germany marched through that country to avoid the defensives lines in the Ardennes, Britain and her Commonwealth states became directly involved. Other countries joined the fray to claim back lost lands and to settle old scores, often resulting in genocide, ethnic cleansing and atrocities on a scale that we will never be able to accurately measure.

Such was the war to end all wars.

CONTENTS

CHAPTER 01: YOUR COUNTRY NEEDS YOU	11
CHAPTER 02: PALS TOGETHER	15
CHAPTER 03: FRIEND OR FOE	27
CHAPTER 04: FRITZ VON FRANKE	35
CHAPTER 05: 'DON'T SHOOT, I'M ENGLISH'	43
CHAPTER 06: SERGEANT JACK JACKSON (NZEF)	48
CHAPTER 07: RESCUE FROM THE ARGONNE FOREST	52
CHAPTER 08: DELIVERING BAD NEWS	65
CHAPTER 09: BURIAL RETRIEVAL UNIT (BRU)	68
THE END OF THE WAR	73
CHAPTER 10: CELEBRATIONS	75
CHAPTER 11: YVETTE AND CELINE	79
CHAPTER 12: FLAVIGNY	86
CHAPTER 13: JON	90
CHAPTER 14: DELLE	96
CHAPTER 15: PARIS NIGHTCLUB	102
CHAPTER 16: ARTUR	107
CHAPTER 17: MICHEL ETXARRI	112
CHAPTER 18: REMEMBRANCE	115
CHAPTER 19: GEORGE MILLS	123
CHAPTER 20: WER BIST DU / WHO ARE YOU?	127

CHAPTER 21: LEAVING DELLE	133
CHAPTER 22: HERBERT SMITH	136
CHAPTER 23: THE SEARCH FOR DESERTERS	138
CHAPTER 24: PARIS	141
CHAPTER 25: WASTED JOURNEY	146
CHAPTER 26: JOSEPH VAN DE VELDT	149
CHAPTER 27: THE CHARGES AGAINST PRIVATE FRED MILLS	154
CHAPTER 28: REVISITING THE BATTLE SITE	160
CHAPTER 29: PREPARATION FOR THE COURT MARTIAL	163
CHAPTER 30: THE COURT MARTIAL – PROSECUTION	166
CHAPTER 31: MOTHERS OF THE FALLEN (MOTF)	171
CHAPTER 32: THE COURT MARTIAL – CHARGES AGAINST PRIVATE FRED MILLS	175
CHAPTER 33: THE COURT MARTIAL – DEFENCE	178
CHAPTER 34: THE COURT MARTIAL – SUMMING UP	183
CHAPTER 35: THE COURT MARTIAL – TOWARDS A CONCLUSION	191
CHAPTER 36: THE COURT MARTIAL – THE VERDICT	201
CHAPTER 37: THE GREAT ESCAPE	205
CHAPTER 38: CONCLUSION	209
DEDICATION	213

CHAPTER 01:

YOUR COUNTRY NEEDS YOU

Mary Anne Mills leant over the dividing wall between the terraced houses in Kempsey Street, Chadderton to attract the attention of her neighbour.

'Have you seen that bloody big poster at the side of the town hall, Alice?'

'That fellow staring at you?' replied her neighbour. 'I've not seen it Mary Anne, but, I've heard about it and it's a disgrace; encouraging these young lads to go fighting in France to save the necks of the French from being overrun by the Germans! To be honest with you, Mary Anne, I don't give a fig about the French. I mean what have the French ever done for us I'd like to know?'

Mary Anne folded her arms to emphasise her point. 'And now we have that Lord Kitchener fellow telling our lads to go and fight Germans. I wouldn't know a German if I fell over one. And between you and me, our William, who reads books and listens to the wireless every night, he says that our king and all his lot are actually German. What do you make of that, Alice?'

Alice nodded in agreement. Not one to ever disagree with her neighbour, sister and best friend.

Monday is washing day and along with the graft of washing, rinsing and mangling sheets, it was time for a good chin wag: a bit of a gossip about people doing things they shouldn't be doing and catching up on any interesting news. The kettle and the largest pan had been put on the black iron cooking range with a fire blazing away underneath to boil the water. The dolly tub, the posset and the washboard were brought out and the weekly process got underway come rain or shine.

The ladies had both married into the Mills family, wives to brothers Fred and Aaron and were as close as sisters. They were friends when there was need of a shoulder to cry on, drinking companions when the opportunity arose for them to leave the children and go and have a tipple and a sing song at one of the local pubs, and confidants when they had a problem, usually to do with their husbands. But they enjoyed nothing more than their time together on Mondays doing their weekly wash.

Mary Anne pulled her face at the site of Fred's long johns. 'I'll tell you what, Alice, that Lord Kitchener fellow should get off his arse and go and fight these foreigners himself instead of encouraging our boys to go fighting for something that's none of our business. My father had seen enough fighting against them Boers a good few years ago. He told me that they were a nasty piece of work. And before that he was fighting them black fellows in the middle of darkest Africa.'

Alice scrubbed away on some woolly socks that were more hole than sock.

'Our George is talking about joining up with some of the lads from the mill and a couple of lads from his old school. Fighting Germans! Huh! He should be fighting off young girls at his age. I remember my Aaron chasing me down the canal when we started courting. I could run faster than him but I slowed down a bit to let him catch me and catch me he did. Now he couldn't catch a cold. All he does when he finishes work is go to Hunt Lane Tavern with your Fred, playing dominoes. He says he only has a couple of pints, but you know fair well that they are lying. At first, it's all lovey-dovey with them coming straight home from work, a quick tea and then an early night That's only until you get a bun in the oven. Now the only thing that stirs him is an empty stomach! Then he downs his pints and hurries home, as nice as nine pence.'

'They are all the same,' commented Mary Anne.

'God forbid, if our George joins up!' Alice exclaimed. 'Your Fred will want to follow suit, mark my words.'

'Thick as thieves, those two.' Mary Anne nodded. 'Our Fred has always hung on to the shirt tails of your George. I'll tell you what, Alice, if our Fred talks about joining up when he's old enough, then I'll kick his arse all the way up Queens Street, and beyond.'

Mary Anne smiled at Alice. 'Talking about Queen Street, I heard that your George is sweet on that young lass from the chippy. She's a bonny girl, no doubt, but she can't fry fish to save her life. Your George's better off playing with her instead of playing soldiers with some foreigners. Leave them who caused the war to fight the war and let our lads grow up on their own without interference from some London toffs playing soldiers.'

Mary Anne pulled a face as she recollected the euphoria in the air after war was declared. 'They said that this war would be over by Christmas.' She sighed. 'Now it's Easter and nothing is happening. I heard a man say that both sides were dug in. I thought "dug in what?" It sounds to me like they are dug into a pile of shit. Ellen Anne from Clough Terrace heard that her sister's boy had copped it in somewhere called Wipers. Apparently he got his head blew off by a shell. Poor lad wouldn't have felt a thing. Well, we had better get on Alice or we'll get nothing done today and if you hear anything you let me know and please keep a grip on your George with him talking soldiers to our Fred. His brain's not set yet so he's easily influenced and he worships your George.'

Saturday afternoon, after work, George came home, quickly washed and put on his best Sunday clothes.

'Where are you off to, our George?' his mother said, half thinking that he would be taking his girlfriend, Annie, to the afternoon matinée at the Roxy picture house.

'I'm off to join up, Mother. I am not being humiliated yet again by one of those girls going about with white feathers. Annie has agreed that we will get married the first time that I am home on leave.'

CHAPTER 02:
PALS TOGETHER

The war progressed slowly and it soon became clear that it was not going to be over by Christmas. The winter of 1914/15 saw the battle lines formed as both sides 'dug in'. The number of casualties increased rapidly as both sides made excursions into the opposing battle lines in the attempt to take some precious ground but such high casualty rates meant the warlords had to review their recruitment policy.

The response to the Kitchener's 'Your Country Needs You' posters exceeded expectations. The concept of the Pals Battalions encouraged large numbers of friends, work mates and school pals to join up together. No thought was given to life and limb and the euphoria of an adventure in a new land captured the imagination of groups of lads who had never travelled more than fifty miles beyond their front doors before. Up to this point, a trip to Blackpool on a charabanc for the lads living in one of the Lancashire cotton mill towns, or a trip to Scarborough for the lads working in the Yorkshire woollen mills, was the highlight of the year and the only sort of adventure they could ever expect.

The formation of the Oldham Pals whetted the appetite of the likes of George Mills and the teenage and early twenties lads working and living in Chadderton near Oldham. The idea spread by word of mouth within the cotton mills, the Boys Brigade, the Scouts and other organisations with a male-orientated outlook. Joining the adventure to fight in a distant land became the thing to do.

The day George got ready in his Sunday best, the lads from around Chadderton had arranged to meet at the local town hall between 1 pm and 3 pm, which allowed some lads to pop in the Sun Inn for a pint or two. As the numbers increased, an air of comradeship gained momentum around those waiting to set off on the march up to Oldham Town Hall. Jim Shelley, the son of the manager of the Manor Mill, which was the largest of the fine spinners in the area, had organised the lads from a disordered muddle into a 'four in a row' orderly group of young, disciplined, soldiers to be. Over one hundred young men marched up Middleton Road to meet up with other local groups. Pals together. Lads from St Luke's School who had scrapped with lads from Derby Street School were now united in a cause. Jim Jones who had been cock of St Luke's School had his arm around John Shaw, the softest lad at school, known as a 'mard arse' who had skriked his eyes out if one of the bigger lads had said boo to him; but now he was ready for an adventure and ready to fight side by side with the local hard case, his new 'pal'.

A crowd of onlookers cheered the lads up the hill to Oldham centre and a large crowd of older men, exempt from the call up, together with women and children cheered the lads as they queued up to sign their names to this crusade into foreign lands.

Annie, from the Queens Road Chippy, had come up town early to get a good view of the lads and her face beamed with pride when she saw her love, George. When they had strolled along the canal the previous Thursday, she had promised George she would show him something nice after he had signed up. George had smiled innocently as though he had no idea what she meant.

But the 'something nice' paled into insignificance as George arrived home later on that Saturday and his mother greeted him with a hefty swipe across his face before hugging him for what he had done.

The overwhelming response to the call for Pals Battalions resulted in a huge swell of numbers eager to fight but there had been a major under-estimation of the resources needed to provide uniforms, to organise billeting locations and to generally have the ability to look after and manage the mass of young lads who had queued up to take the king's shilling. After going through the so-called medical, a local field became the temporary home of the 'Pals'. The limited number of tents meant that many slept outside with only a couple of blankets for warmth and comfort.

The lack of officers was soon highlighted as a major problem. The solution was found in young gentlemen from the upper echelons of society. Gentlemen brought up by a 'nanny' and educated in so-called 'public schools.' These were the 'men' considered to have the backbone and discipline to manage groups of working class lads. They remained aloof from their charges and in doing so helped create the illusion that they had the mettle to lead from the front. Many did lead from the front and paid the price for the bravery shown.

The training to make fighting men from raw lads took several stages at various locations. Initially the lads from Oldham were billeted at tented camps set up in the local parks. The Oldham Pals worked hard to show their superiority over the other Pals and a competitive spirit soon developed. The sergeant in charge thought that a boxing competition would bring unity to the differing local groups and lads were matched up evenly against each other based on height and weight.

The Oldham Pals thought they had a champion in Jim Jones, the ex cock of Derby Street School. He was matched against a similar sized lad from Salford but didn't even last the first of the three five-minute rounds. Amongst the lightweights, Skriker Shaw, a skinny lad from Freehold, took a pasting in the first two rounds of his match and nearly broke out crying. Encouraged by his Oldham Pals, he held on and seemed to develop a second wind for the third round. He said to himself, 'I've got this far, I am going to do my best for the lads.' He finished up giving his opponent from Cheetham Hill a good hiding and won the match with a knock out at the end of the third round. Cheers thundered for Skriker and he went on to fight the next round against a much bigger lad from Swinton. Instead of facing up against his opponent he danced around the 'ring' then picked his chance to give the other lad a left hook which left his opponent with a black eye and bloody nose. Through the semi-final and another knock out, he found himself in the final against a whippet of a lad from Salford docks who had given each of his previous opponents a good leathering. Skriker danced through the first two rounds without throwing a punch; he had developed a unique technique throughout the competition, using speed and movement and saving all his energy for that final meaningful punch. The third round saw the Salford lad tired out from chasing Skriker round the ring and one punch from the Oldham lad finished him off.

John Shaw, alias the Skriker, went from zero to hero, becoming 'champion boxer' throughout the army training programme in several locations up and down the country. John's sergeant major trained him as he could see a long-term future for both John Shaw and himself on the boxing circuit providing he could keep the unwelcome interests of some of the army officers at bay.

For the first time in his young life John (the Dancer) Shaw was wanted.

During the intense training programme the Oldham Pals were taught discipline, tactics, hand-to-hand fighting and before long they were ready for action.

Initially the lads became attached to a reserve unit whose duty was to replace the 'fallen' and injured in whatever infantry unit needed them. Many became attached to the Duke of Cornwall's Light Infantry as replacements for the tremendous losses that unit, amongst others, had suffered on the 1st July 1916, the first day of the Battle of the Somme.

The Oldham Pals knew that, even after the training and fighting bags of straw suspended on a wooden frame by rope, fighting the Hun would be far from a stroll in the park.

At the end of a long day's travel they reached the rear assembly area just before midnight. They missed the sight of trucks taking away dead bodies from both sides to a burial site some five miles away to the rear. What the lads did hear was the sound of some poor lads shouting and screaming for their mothers. The shouting would carry on for a few hours then stop. Maybe the poor lads had got some sleep. More likely they had succumbed to injuries. Word of mouth informed the new front-line soldiers that the army had lost tens of thousands of men during the first days of July. Perhaps it would calm down a bit.

Within the Oldham Pals, smaller groups of close mates formed. These mates may have been cousins, neighbours, brothers, school friends or just some lads who got on with each other. Four lads who had stuck together were George Mills, Jim Jones, John Richards and John (the Dancer) Shaw: no longer the Skriker. He was the hero of the Oldham Pals and officers had indicated that when he got home on leave he would be entered into a preliminary competition to fight for the army boxing championship. If successful, there was talk amongst the officers of backing John to go professional. Word of mouth from the senior officers at HQ instructed the line of command to 'keep that skinny lad from Oldham out of harm's way'. But John Shaw would stick with his three mates through thick and thin. George, who was promoted to lance corporal, would himself keep an eye on John.

The four lads soon got involved in the horrors of war. They knew fear when they learnt that the next day would see them on the front line. They felt the anticipation, in those few minutes before the captain blew his whistle, when you looked right then left at your close mates, wondering whether this was it: the end. They experienced euphoria as the day ended and their objective had been achieved. They also knew the joy of being back together again, recalling the luck that had followed them that day, smiling with relief that they had come through the day's carnage unscathed while keenly feeling the loss of fellow soldiers, slaughtered in horrific circumstances.

Day's came and went: days on the front line doing nothing except hoping a German shell didn't come your way; days in the reserve trench chatting about nothing and days in the back trenches counting the days until a trip home was on the horizon.

Eventually the sergeant's voice boomed, 'Mills, Jones, Shaw and Richards. You four good for nothings can get your arses out of France and tell the world of all the good times that you have been having.'

They marched out of the rear lines to the trucks waiting to take the lucky ones to the trains at Calais or Dieppe. They spent the hour or so on the boat back to Blighty being seasick. Then it was a train to London, a train to Manchester, the local train to Werneth and, finally, a two mile walk home.

'What do I do?' George pondered. 'Do I go to Annie's at the chippy or do I go home? I know, I'll go and see Annie first, just for a minute, then go home, then back to see Annie.'

'Come home with me, John,' George said to 'the Dancer'. 'Annie has a little sister, not so little now, I guess, but she would suit you and according to Annie's letters, she is not attached.'

George's mother, Alice, cried her eyes out when he turned up out of the blue and in one piece.

'I need to see our Fred. Where is he?' George asked.

'He's doing afternoons at the Manor Mill. He finishes in just over an hour. Go and get Annie and wait at the gates for him,' his mother suggested.

Fred's face beamed as he saw George and Annie; the three just stood there together and hugged. Fred wanted to tell George that, being eighteen, he had been called up for service and would be joining the training camp in two weeks. Eventually Fred wanted to join the DCLIs with George, John, Jim and John Richards. He had to tell his mother but that could wait until after the wedding so as not put a damper on the celebrations.

As they walked home George and Annie talked about their swiftly arranged wedding that was to take place at Turf Lane Methodist Church the following Saturday, in just eight days' time. After the ceremony, they were going to stay in Blackpool for three days with two nights spent at a boarding house on Hornby Road.

'Fred,' George started, 'will you do me the honour of being my best man? I've asked John Shaw to be my usher in church. That way he'll be able to make the acquaintance of Annie's sister, Helen.'

The wedding went ahead as planned. The bride and groom took the train to Blackpool changing at Manchester, Wigan and Preston before finally arriving Blackpool Central, a short walk from Hornby Road. The war effort had prioritised trains for more pressing needs than a young couple's first night together.

John and Helen hit it off straight away but John was visibly upset when the other three lads got their return papers and John was asked to meet a professional man in the Midland Hotel, having been told he should bring either his mother or girl with him.

Frederick H Rogers was a well-known promoter on the London boxing scene and, through his many contacts, he was aware of the skill and unique ability of John (The Dancer) Shaw. He offered to fund a training programme for John in anticipation of the commencement of sporting activities as soon as the war was over. Clean digs in North London were offered to the couple that would commence in three weeks.

'You'd better get a ring on that young ladies finger, John, if we are to go ahead with this plan,' suggested the promoter.

Mr Rogers handed John Shaw a roll of one pound and ten shilling notes to pay for the wedding. Both families were over the moon at the couple's good fortune. The wedding of John and Helen was as extravagant as any other mill worker's that had taken place before the war. But, there was a sadness hanging over John because his three close friends could not be with them; a sadness Annie shared due to her husband, George, not being able to stand by her side on this happy day.

The new found fame of John (the Dancer) Shaw had not gone un-noticed amongst the people of Chadderton. As the couple left the church for a sit down meal in the function room of the Radclyffe Arms, where they were to be entertained by the Nimble Nook Brass Band, it was noted that John, through his boxing escapades, had certainly made his mark in life. After a week's honeymoon in a sea-view room at the St George's Hotel in Llandudno, it was back to his new home in the back bedroom of Helen's parent's chippy.

Mr Rogers had arranged a series of exhibition bouts for his boxers, focusing on the southern ports of England, to entertain troops who had travelled thousands of miles from the outposts of the British Empire: New Zealand, Australia, South Africa and India, with the addition of some of the local regiments that were on leave.

The first venue, in Portsmouth, was a great success with six exhibition bouts from Flyweight to Light Heavyweight, showcasing boxers from the Roger's Stable against local and invited opponents.

John 'the Dancer' Shaw was one of the most popular boxers and, from being the first bout on the card became the most popular one, due to his unique approach to the job in hand. The next exhibition bouts were to take place in Southampton and Plymouth before being 'top of the bill' at the major training camp on Salisbury Plain. The final venue was to be at the town hall in Bristol, before returning home to cook and serve fish and chips in between guest boxing experiences in and around Lancashire. The chippy quadrupled in business once the word was out that 'the Dancer' was working the batter, salt and vinegar.

John and Helen caught a train from Plymouth to Exeter along with troops who had landed two days previously and the train was packed. Some of the New Zealanders recognised John and insisted that John and his wife join them in one of the carriages. The soldiers had been told that, at the first stop, they could disembark to collect some food and provisions that had been arranged for them. An unscheduled stop at a local station caused troops to assume that they had reached Exeter. The troops in the carriage around John and Helen disembarked on the same side that they had entered the train and John and Helen joined them.

The Plymouth to London express train came around the bend at 50 mph and the driver had no time to apply his brakes before hitting a small group of people who were on the wrong side of the train. John and Helen were amongst the fifteen people who died instantly.

The train disaster made front page news, the newspapers all assuming that the dead and injured were from New Zealand.

The welcoming committee at Salisbury started to wonder if the boxer and his wife had been somehow affected by the rail disaster that had closed the line for over a day while investigating authorities carried out their duties. As night fell, and there was no sight of John and Helen. It started to dawn that the young couple had possibly been among those directly involved. The chief of police in Exeter confirmed that two civilians, a young man and a young lady, were among the deceased. The message was relayed to Lancashire Police in Manchester, who sent two senior officers to Queen Street to relay the sad news.

The town of Oldham went into shock; it was as though two of the Pals' leading soldiers had been killed. Oldham had become used to bad news but the death of this popular young couple united the whole community in grief.

The young couple's families were devastated and could not be consoled, but it was decided to withhold the news from George and his two close friends for a short time.

Around the time of the train disaster in September 1917, the three friends were on the front line waiting for the signal to go over the top in a planned attack on Polygon Wood located in West Flanders near to Ypres, a town that had been the scene of intense fighting for most of the war. The area had been under the control of the German army since 1915 and the DCLI were amongst troops from East Lancashire, New Zealand and Australia ready for action.

George was pulled from the front line by his captain to be told the sad news about his best friend and his sister-in-law. During the advance into German territory and under intense fighting George lost his two close friends, Jim Jones and John Richards.

Within a week the four friends had become one. George Mills.

George was seen by army leadership as an experienced soldier who had been promoted to lance corporal. He continued to serve his unit and, due to the sad news of his friends and family, he showed little concern for his own safety. Part of his duty was to be responsible for the induction of new recruits, most of them still 'wet behind the ears'. Without his guidance they would have become mere cannon-fodder, just like thousands of young lads and men before them.

George was summoned to see the battalion colonel for what George assumed was to be a man-to-man talk about his recent losses. He was passed a list of new recruits to see if he recognised any of the names.

And there was the name of Fred Mills, DCLI 30103.

George was joyful at the thought of meeting up with Fred but his joy was tinged with sadness as he considered what Fred was about to see and experience.

The war moved to a virtual stalemate with each side making excursions into enemy territory but with both having mixed success with this tactic. What the front line feared most was the threat from German snipers. George had given a talk to the new lads and Fred, in particular, about what damage these skilled, highly trained and patient marksmen could do.

Luckily for many young recruits, these snipers wanted to kill off officers to boost their credibility rather than take out a young Tommy, and once a sniper had released his deadly bullet, he could be instantly located, identified and targeted.

During the early months of 1918 when the Germans threw all their resources at the British sector in an attempt to break the deadlock. The United States of America had entered the war and the German generals anticipated that the addition of these fresh troops would have a detrimental effect on the war plans of the German Empire. The plan had been, and as far as the German generals were concerned still was, to target and outflank the British troops in the Somme region and break through to the English Channel. But the initial impact from Ludendorff's army could not be maintained because of issues with the supply of food and ammunition to the forward troops. Their assault soon lost impetus and, by the end of June, the German army had lost all of the ground captured in the previous weeks leaving them in retreat, causing major problems with morale, which resulted in significant numbers of desertions.

Fred and George fought together throughout the first six months of 1918 but, during the summer months, George was requested to impart knowledge of his front-line experience to newly arrived troops from New Zealand. Fred continued to serve with the DCLI, planning and training for a final assault on the German army. A wide frontal attack on the German defensive lines was planned for late summer intended to be the final thrust to end the war and send the troops home. All planned leave was cancelled just two days away from when the Mills cousins were due to take a fortnight's leave from the fight for freedom.

All training and resources focused on a concentrated push to take the Hindenburg Line: the first line of defence of the German army. The German hierarchy insisted that this line must be upheld and mustn't, under any circumstances, be breached. They knew that to lose this strategic position would lead to their ultimate defeat.

CHAPTER 03:
FRIEND OR FOE

'Piece a piss! That's what it'll be, lads: a piece of piss.'

This was how the sergeant explained the plan to his men. 'Them Germans won't know what's hit 'em once we start firing them heavy guns. They'll be blown to smithereens with bits of them all over the place. All we have to do is go over the top, finish off some poor sod who's still breathing, collect a few mementoes, then it's a gentle stroll in the park to take that Hindenburg Line. Once we are in shooting distance of the Line they will come out of their tunnels and throw themselves at our mercy. They will pack up and the war will be over. We might have to take a few out for good measure but I suppose we have to respect the white flag. Like I said, lads, it's a piece of piss.'

Sergeant James MacTavish had seen it all. He had joined up in 1890 as a sixteen-year-old lad and had fought in wars and skirmishes all over the globe to protect the pink bits of the world map. The next day, the 29 September 1918, was to be his last day in combat. He'd done his bit for king and country and had spent the best part of four years fighting the Hun. The officers had informed the troops under their command that this was to be the final push. One last effort and then the boys can go home.

'All us front line troops have to do,' McTavish enthused, 'is to walk to the German lines, take a few prisoners, shoot a few who look suspicious and that will be all. The war will be over, the Hun will surrender and we can start to think about going home.'

'Weren't we told four years ago that it would be all over by Christmas?' muttered a soldier.

McTavish nodded. He had spent four wasted years fighting the square heads. Time he could have spent watching the world go by at his home on the island of Mull. He would have said hello to passing islanders, exchanged a few pleasantries with neighbours and at five o'clock, he would have downed his first pint in the public bar in that big hotel, on the hill, overlooking Tobermory. Perhaps, occasionally, he could have taken hotel guests out fishing or on a day trip to one of the islands of the Inner Hebrides: Coll or Islay.

One hundred or so yards back towards the Hindenburg Line, a camouflaged Herbert Schultz was waiting; an experienced member of the German army's Sniper Division. Members of this unit were a dedicated, highly trained group of expert marksmen who had rifles fixed with long distance scopes so they could pick out any enemy soldier who got careless enough to put his head into view.

Herbert knew that this was to be his last day on earth.

He had spent several months in training. He had sought out dens to hide in and had the patience to wait until an officer or a soldier of influence came, even for a split second, into his sights. There was no point taking out a rank and file soldier; the special bullet had to kill and kill meaningfully. He had a special skill, a skill that had taken months of training, a skill that marked out the German snipers from their British counterparts. The British relied on 'good shots': shots that could kill an elephant at point blank range or excel in a clay pigeon competition, but the British snipers had no surveillance skills; no training in patience. They were just good shots.

Herbert hated his role as sniper and felt sorry for his intended victims, as they had little chance of survival once he had got them in his sights.

From his vantage point he had a clear view of the British front line and, as the dawn mist cleared, he sensed that something was about to happen from the British lines. With his Carl Zeiss binoculars he searched the top of the British trench to see if there was any small hole or perhaps a missing divot that would give him a chance to show off his skills.

Herbert did not have a care for the rest of his own unit or what might happen to them when the inevitable happened and the British won the war. He had served the kaiser for nearly three years fighting in this war that had become a living hell.

Should he stay and carry out his duty or should he abandon his post and take his chance with the victors? It was an empty question because he knew that he would stay and do what he had to do.

Herbert thought he could see a tiny movement at the top of the British trench and with his binoculars he noticed a tiny gap in a grass sod. Enough to get a bullet in if someone passed the spot. On closer observation he spotted a red beard passing too. If the red beard passed by again, he would have him.

Just as Herbert expected, the barrage of heavy guns started the moment the mist cleared. God help his friends when the shells hit; they would be blown to bits: skin and bone, gristle and flesh.

The opportunity he had been waiting for came quickly. The red beard passed the hole and within a split second his head was blown apart. Red beard would have had no idea what had hit him. No pain, no last breath, just peace with his maker.

Herbert's joy, however, was short lived as his position was quickly identified and a twelve-pound shell sent him to join red beard in Heaven or Hell, Paradise or Purgatory. Two professional soldiers were gone within moments of each other. Men who, in another life and in different circumstances, might have been friends, but it was dog eat dog, fighting for their countries; fighting for the king, fighting for the kaiser.

Perhaps the two grandsons of the British queen should have had a duel at dawn instead of inflicting five years of stalemated conflict.

On the front line, British trench Sargent James (Jock) McTavish had just distributed a tot of rum to his troops. 'This'll keep you warm when you march to victory, lads. It'll be a piece of p—'

But the 'iss' did not get out of his mouth before his head disappeared in a red mist.

Jock was no more.

No more pints of heavy in his engraved tankard kept especially for him at the Rob Roy Bar in the Western Isles Hotel.

No more sailing to the Inner Islands with his dog Jimmy.

No more camaraderie in the sergeants' mess at HQ in Glasgow.

If only he had had another second of time, he could have passed that small gap in the trench wall and lived to tell the tale.

The sight of the sergeant's limp, headless body galvanised the troops as they prepared for the whistle from Captain Stephen. Those closest to their Scottish 'father figure' were visibly shocked at the unfairness of this terrible conflict and, as the order came to fix bayonets, the troops just wanted revenge and they wanted it the moment they got sight of any member of the enemy. Not that they expected to see anything left of the Hun after the incessant barrage of guns had, no doubt, cleared the enemy lines of any threat.

Fred Mills' regiment, the Duke of Cornwall's Light Infantry, had been part of the Third Army under the leadership of Sir Julian Byng and had been fighting alongside troops from Lancashire and New Zealand, with whom Fred had formed a close attachment.

They had been based near to Perone after the town had been captured from the German army at the end of August. The momentum now was to push the Hun back to their defensive lines and beyond. The breaching of the Hindenburg Line was given priority importance as the generals considered that the capture of such a strategic defensive position would be the beginning of the end for the demoralised German troops.

From the reserve trenches, Fred and his colleagues reached their front-line position in readiness for going over the top just after the break of dawn on the 29 September 1918. The order was to advance and take the village of La Vacquerie, and, after consolidating their gains and organising themselves for further action, they were to carry on to towards the St Quentin Canal, that being a strategic part of the German defensive system.

After taking this important defence, the German army would, according to the Allied leadership, surrender. The war would be over. The war would be won.

The time for action came. The brief warmth from the rum dissipated as the whistle sounded and the troops climbed the fire step into an eerie silence as they started their move forward.

Fred and his close comrades hesitated slightly as they moved forward away from the relative safety of the complex trench system, a place that had become 'home' for the last three days while they waited for action.

Where was the Hun?

Had they been wiped out?

The troops had moved about 200 yards when all of a sudden, a great cacophony of rattling machine guns cut through the ranks. Fred Mills saw men mown down on either side of him. The men who had run in front of him, in an attempt to be the first to the enemy lines, were no more. Men behind him fell but Fred kept going. There was nowhere to hide from the bullets, many of them whistling past his ear to catch the poor sod behind him.

Realising that the front-line troops were getting killed and injured without any benefit or gains, a signal was sent to the gun command to reset the guns to a deeper position due to the infantry having advanced further than predicted. But a miscalculation of the signal resulted in the shells falling on their own troops who had travelled the farthest forward.

Men fell in front of Fred both from enemy fire and now friendly fire. A total disaster was avoided as some troops managed to get to enemy trenches and engage in hand-to-hand fighting with bayonets, pistols and the odd trenching shovel. This weapon turned out to be more effective than the bayonet as a full swing of the shovel could take off a Hun's head.

The ruthless effectiveness of the British attack signalled to many German defenders that fighting was futile and it would be more sensible to make a run for it rather than be killed in the trenches. The German officers tried to stem the flow of deserting soldiers by ordering them to stiffen up and face the enemy but the demand fell on deaf ears as the attempt to hold their ground became futile. The British Tommys swiftly took control and showed no sympathy to what were mainly youths, just out of school, drafted into forward positions, while the more experienced soldiers manned the deeper and more secure second line defending the Hindenburg Line.

After taking control of the enemy forward positions the British troops came under intense fire, which held up the advance. Fred was in a group of soldiers gaining ground and moving from shell hole to shell hole making progress toward a machine gun position partially hidden in what was the remains of an orchard. Moving forward in a battle that had no defensive line or attacking position, the conflict became a shambles with friend and foe dying together with injured men from both sides lying side by side on the battlefield.

Eventually Fred and a group of Australians made it unscathed to the remains of the orchard wall and successfully took out the machine gun position. As he was pushing forward, he came across Captain

Stephen lying partially submerged in a water-filled shell hole. With the help of an Australian comrade, Fred pulled his captain out of the quagmire.

Fred told the Australian that he would check the extent of the captain's injuries and would stay with him to keep him calm until help came from the medical corps.

He had been acting as batman to Captain Stephen during the weeks building up to the push forward and the two men had developed a mutual respect for each other. The relationship between the two went as far as Fred being invited to Captain Stephen's wedding to his fiancé, Mavis, an event that was supposed to be taking place during the next period of leave after the push on the Hindenburg Line.

Having had some first aid training on the battlefield Fred realised that the Captain had suffered a serious stomach injury. Captain Stephen ordered Fred to leave him for the medics and to take his satchel, containing his orders, to the sergeant in charge, which should have been MacTavish but failing that, it was to be given to a junior officer. 'And Fred,' he said quietly, 'if I don't get out of here, tell Mavis that I love her.'

Fred was joined by a colleague, who had recently joined the DCLI, and had spent time training as a 'helper' in a casualty clearing station. Fred told him to stay with the captain while he carried out the captain's orders to take the satchel to the first officer he encountered. Shortly after Fred left the shell hole, the captain succumbed to his injuries.

Fred soon caught up with the attacking Allies and passed the satchel to the sergeant in charge of the sector. Fred and the sergeant and two other soldiers cautiously moved forward towards the enemy lines but as the vista became poor due to a combination of the mist, the featureless landscape and the indiscriminate use of mustard gas, the group became separated. The sergeant's shout of 'Fred' was followed by two shots. German soldiers, who had advanced into the British forward lines under the cover of poor visibility, were able to take out random Allied troops. Fred kept his head down and his rifle at the ready as the Germans took the satchel from the dead sergeant and retreated towards their own lines.

Moving forward the three became under attack from shells fired indiscriminative towards the attacking forces. One shell landed to the left of the group resulting in both soldiers taking the brunt of the force, partially sheltering Fred from the direct impact but resulting in him becoming stunned losing his hearing and orientation. Fred lay in the mud next to the arms and legs of one of his colleagues and it took some time for Fred to realise that he was still in one piece. By that time the attack had moved forward and reached the main German defence position.

Fred was on his own.

CHAPTER 04:
FRITZ VON FRANKE

In the German reserve trenches, just forward of the canal, Fritz von Franke was waiting for the inevitable shell to fly over from the British trenches and end his short life.

Morale was low in the German ranks. It had been since the previous spring, when the push from the German army had petered out and the British and Allied forces had taken the initiative. Germany had seen many successes during the early part of 1918 and it had looked, at one point, as though the Germans would march into Paris.

That was then, but, suddenly, the boot was on the other foot as the Allies sensed victory and a victory that would come soon. The German High Command could not come up with a viable solution and mutterings started, to the effect that they should end the war on the best possible terms.

Fritz thought it ironic that he was to be to be killed, or at best seriously injured by his native brothers. His mind wandered back to how he had come to be in his current predicament.

Fritz was British, English by birth, Lancastrian by county and an Oldhamer. The comfortable living in Manchester had ended at the outbreak of the present conflict. His father, Alfred, a textile machinery expert, had been posted to Lancashire by his German bosses to oversee the installation of carding and ring spinning equipment in some of the dozens of cotton mills in the Oldham, Bolton and Rochdale area.

Alfred, had met his wife, Ethel, while he was working at the Lily Mill in Shaw. Ethel had been a Doffer in the ring room and was over the moon to be asked for a date by this very attractive, blond foreigner who told people that he was Alsatian, not German. Not that anyone understood the significance of the fact that the Alsace was French until the defeat of the French by their German neighbours in 1870. Fritz (known as Francis in English) was brought up in Werneth, one of the better areas of Oldham, and enjoyed spending his childhood in the local Werneth Park, just on his doorstep.

His mother stayed at home with Fritz, who was born in 1900, and he had an idyllic upbringing with his two younger sisters. At home the primary language was English and the three children spoke it perfectly with just a slight guttural accent, the result of having to speak German when their father was home.

Alfred, Fritz's father, had no interest in politics and knew little of the significance of the news coming from Austria that some young man had shot and killed some prince, the next in line to the Austro-Hungarian Empire.

It came as a total shock when Alfred was called to the boardroom of the Manor Mill in Chadderton, where he was carrying out the final acceptance checks on a complete installation of carding equipment. He was confronted by three police officers of differing ranks, the senior introducing himself as chief constable. Joining the policemen was the managing director of the Mill, James Dawson. The chief constable explained that, due to worsening relations between Britain and Germany, Alfred must leave the country at once and return to Germany with his family. Alfred's shock at this news was echoed by James Dawson, who informed the police officers that Alfred could not leave as he had to complete the installation of the equipment he had purchased to increase the capacity of Manor Mill.

The chief constable informed them that his office had arranged for a transport company to collect Alfred and his family in three days' time and that the transport arrangements would only allow personal effects limited to two large suitcases for the parents and a small to medium sized case for each of the children. The officer explained that the Manor Mill Company must pay the equivalent of three months' salary to Alfred then claim the money back from the German company through an arrangement to be made by the Foreign Office. The cost of transportation would be met by His Majesty's Government, under an exchange arrangement that allowed British subjects residing in Germany to return back to the British isles.

Fritz and his family were then to be aided by the German authorities who had organised temporary accommodation in Colmar, in the Alsace region.

By the end of spring 1915 the von Franke family had settled in Mulhouse, known as the German Manchester, and Alfred quickly found employment in a large armament factory where he soon made the rank of overseer of the milling section.

Back in Oldham, on reaching his fourteenth birthday, Fritz had started Technical College in Openshaw, Manchester, to study mechanical design. Here, he had gained initial training in the subject, including complex component design, which should, in theory, have given him some advantage when applying to further his education in Germany.

In Germany, at an interview for a position as apprentice designer, the chief designer explained to Fritz how British engineering was years behind German engineering and that he would be best served getting shop floor experience in turning and milling then perhaps moving into the design department later. Fritz accepted this reasoning and eagerly awaited confirmation from the factory about the proposed apprenticeship, which would commence the following September. In the meantime, Fritz took a temporary job as bicycle delivery boy for the town's largest butcher. In anticipation of receiving a letter from the company, he had been first to the post box each morning.

On the 30th August 1916, however, he received not one, but two official looking letters. As he opened the first, he was overcome with joy as it confirmed his position of apprentice engineer from the 10th September 1916. He rushed to give his mother a hug.

'Open the other letter, let's see what that is,' his mother said.

Fritz did just that but, as he read the contents, his heart fell. He had been called up for training in the Black Forest for the infantry division commencing 1st December 1916 for six months until June 1917 and from there he would be allocated to an infantry unit. Third class rail warrants were enclosed together with further instructions as to the location of the training camp.

Fritz's first taste of the conflict was on the 8th August 1918, as part of the German 2nd Army who suffered humiliating defeats to mainly French and American troops around the town of Chateau-Thierry.

The German army had to retreat, thus giving up the positions they had taken during their offensive the previous three months. Fritz had seen his comrades and fellow novice soldiers decimated by superior soldiers employing superior tactics driving the German army back to the east.

Many of his colleagues had questioned his soft accent and noticed that Fritz's command of the German language was somewhat limited. The bravery he had shown on the battlefield, however, and the support he had given to fallen colleagues had endeared him to the rank and file of the division in which he served.

Fritz was given leave for two weeks from mid-August to the end of that month. Like his friends, he spent most of his time drinking, and taking occasional pleasure with ladies offering comfort in hotels in the centre of Stuttgart. His good looks and blonde hair made him popular with the waitresses at the Central Hotel and, even when his money had gone, he was still taken to the private rooms with two or three of his newfound friends.

But this would not last. He steered clear of all the mutterings against the army chiefs and the kaiser, but he knew that the war would end soon and he would be on the losing side. Perhaps his language skills would be of use. He used German everyday but still considered English to be his first language. Perhaps there would be a place for him in England after the war, if he survived.

Living in Alsace from late 1914 to enlistment in 1916 had honed his knowledge of French, which had been a big advantage in wooing the prettier French family daughters who showed much more affection and friendliness than a lot of the German girls. A saying that he had heard his mother say, 'Any port in a storm', just about summed up his leisure time.

Fritz's mother had come by herself to the station when the day had arrived to see him off. The assembly location would only be given once he was on the train and moving. The stories from the front line and the sight of the mutilated soldiers had convinced his mother that Fritz's departure should be low key and that no fuss should be made, which is why his sisters had not come to the station. His father had commitments at the armament factory but he sent Fritz a note wishing him safe conduct and telling his son how fond he was of him.

The army camp was situated about 50 km from the Hindenburg Line, way out of reach of the British artillery. The training focused on improving hand-to-hand fighting, the use of the bayonet and of any other implement that was to hand. The intensity of the training prepared the troops for what was expected to be a blood-soaked contest with no corner given and none taken. Fritz knew that some of his fellow soldiers did not have the balls for the hand-to-hand fighting and that they would never survive a close man-to-man conflict.

The German command had come into possession of a leather satchel containing apparent battle plans for an all-out offensive on the German defence lines, to be carried out during the last week in September and the first week in October, commencing the 29th, but it was subject to some unspecified conditions, to be decided on at a later date.

The highest ranked German commanders were summoned to discuss the validity of these documents and to decide on a course of action. The decision was taken by Erich Ludendorff, the German army chief strategist, to dismiss the plans as hoaxes believing his army should avoid being led by the nose into a trap set up by the British, French and now the Americans.

On the 26th September Fritz's unit moved into the reserve trenches where they would be prepared for action from opposing lines and so be ready to support the soldiers in the forward trenches: the Germans first line of defence. The morning of the 28th saw the start of a great barrage of heavy artillery targeting the German lines. Fritz was stationed on the high ground above and to the side of a small hamlet named La Vacquerie. The barrage seemed to concentrate on buildings in the village and the startled residents took the brunt of it with men, women and children being killed while the German army itself remained intact. Snipers had been stationed at strategic locations with orders to take out any opponent who appeared to be in a position of authority, because without leadership, the Germans presumed the Allied army would be like headless chickens and cannon-fodder for the many machine gun emplacements.

As predicted by the German officers, the whistles were blown just after dawn on the 29th and the British soldiers started their forward action. The troops confidently moved forward from their trench, sustained in the belief that their bombardment had done its job. The only job the Allied bombardment had actually done was to create a landscape that appeared to resemble the craters on the surface of the moon. A small crater would subsequently be made larger and the greatest danger was to fall into one of these massive orifices, because, if that happened, there was no way out of these steep sided shell holes.

The casual walk forward by opposing troops towards Fritz's sector was preceded by a small man in a strange skirt blowing into a bag, which omitted a piercing wailing noise. When Fritz's colleagues opened fire with a hail of automatic fire power the small man was hit with so many bullets he seemed to vaporise.

After the disastrous march forward there was a change in tactic as the British started to cover the area with gunfire. For a split second Fritz felt sorry for the poor soldiers that he was fighting. The bulk of the frontal attack on German lines was caught between the machine gun fire from the German lines and the heavy shells falling on the attackers from their own side. Fritz took careful aim at a soldier so as only to hit him on the shoulder. The force was enough to send the Tommy spinning and Fritz watched him fall into a deep, water-filled shell hole. He could hear the screams from the poor man as he tried to save himself from drowning in the rat-infested cesspit. The screams soon died down and Fritz felt for the soldier as he had suffered a particularly gruesome death. But that was what this war was about. Soldiers on both sides of the barbed wire suffered the same fate. A close colleague of Fritz said he'd had enough and was taking a chance to run while he was still in one piece. As soon as he started to run towards the rear lines, an officer was waiting with his pistol and, without any hesitation, shot the soldier dead. 'Let that be a warning to anyone who is thinking of deserting,' he said.

Fritz was incensed by such a meaningless act of violence from a so-called 'superior' officer who represented the kaiser so, he in turn, shot the officer in the head. He moved quickly away from the scene and soon reached a quieter area where he was able to isolate himself from the onslaught.

CHAPTER 05:
'DON'T SHOOT, I'M ENGLISH'

A soldier, who Fritz knew, ran towards the shallow ditch where he was sheltering, but just as he reached safety, the man took a bullet in his back. Fritz pulled the soldier into the partly covered ditch, which was reasonably well hidden by fallen tree stumps. From the noise of the battlefield it was obvious that the German army was retreating to one their many defensive lines. As his colleague fell into a pain-induced sleep, Fritz put a rag in the soldier's mouth to subdue the noise of his groaning but also to help him stand the pain without biting his tongue off.

Time passed, it was dusk and Fritz had been in the ditch for over five hours. The injured soldier cried out in pain so Fritz pushed the rag deeper into his mouth. All of a sudden, a British soldier appeared with his rifle ready to kill both him and his injured colleague. As he was about to fire, Fritz cried out, 'Don't shoot, I'm English!'

The soldier hesitated and demanded that both soldiers relinquish their weapons, which Fritz did immediately, making sure that his movements were not threatening.

'My colleague is dying,' Fritz began. 'I have left the German positions as I've had enough and wish to be taken prisoner. I prefer to take my chance with the British Army rather than carry on trying to defend the indefensible. I am from the Manchester area and I am English. Born in England and brought up in England. That was until this bloody war'

The British soldier was clearly taken aback with the clarity and sincerity of what this Hun was saying, but a German could never be trusted.

The German attended to his colleague as best he could but it was obvious the soldier was seriously injured. Fred noted the compassion with which this man treated his friend and how there was no display of aggression towards his British captor. As the sky became darker and the sound of the battle became more distant, decisions had to be made. Fred realised that he could not stay in his current position much longer so he considered his choices: he could leave the ditch on his own and walk forward into the sound of gun fire, leaving the two Germans to their fate; he could kill both the Germans and leave the ditch; or he could move away with the English German leaving the other man to die. The decision became clearer when the injured soldier breathed his last.

Night fell and Fred kept his full attention on the remaining German.

'What's your name, German?' Fred asked with authority.

'Fritz von Franke.'

'You say you lived in Manchester? Where did you live and what school did you go to?'

'I was born in Werneth near Oldham. I lived there for my first ten years and, after that, we moved around Stockport, Ashton and Bolton for four years, depending on my father's work requirements. From the age of five I went to Derby Street School in Hollinwood and then to various schools in the areas where we lived.'

'I knew some lads who went to that school. I played against them at football. Did you play for the school?' Fred asked.

'No', Fritz explained, 'the younger boys didn't get a chance to play football until they were ten, but I played for the Stockport boys' team at the age of twelve just before we moved back to Werneth, when my father started working at the Earl Mill.'

Fritz's answers were convincing and eventually both men started reminiscing about the fun they'd had up to leaving school when, in Fred's case, he'd started working part-time at Stocks Mill in Chadderton, working alternate mornings and afternoons as a 'little piercer' mending broken ends by jumping in and out of the spinning machine as it moved forward and backward during its cycle.

'Did you ever go into Manchester and play on the escalator in the big store?' Fred enquired. 'I've forgot the name of it now.'

'You mean Lewis's.' Fritz replied. 'I remember going down Manchester with Tommy Lawson during the summer holidays. I'd be nine years old and Tommy would be about twelve. We walked more than five miles; it took us a couple of hours. We played on the escalator and listened to the brass band play in Piccadilly gardens. One thing I remember clearly is that Tommy had a couple of stink bombs, which he let off at the bottom of the escalator. We laughed and laughed until the store guard collared us and took us to the police box on the corner. The sergeant, who was eating his butty and drinking a large mug of tea, was not very happy when he was disturbed. He gave us both a clip round the ear and told us that if there was a next time he would give us a proper pasting. He asked for our names and addresses then wrote a note and gave it to Tommy telling him to get on the number 82 bus and to hand it to the bus conductor who would give us a free ride to Werneth. My mother was not pleased when I told her what I'd been doing. "I've a good mind to tell your father when he gets home," she scolded.

'I knew she wouldn't,' Fritz said to Fred. 'Our mother protected us children from our father, who was sometimes in a bad mood. He was particularly bad tempered when he came home after working twelve hours a day for six days a week assembling the machines sent from his company in Germany. Most of the time he was working on his own when the promised help from the mill management had disappeared to the local public house.'

Although Fritz's story was strange and complicated, Fred became convinced that this German was telling the truth and, although they were fighting for different countries, it appeared that they had much in common.

'OK,' Fred said. 'My name is Fred Mills and I lived in Kempsey Street, near St. Luke's Church in Chadderton. I believe you are who you say you are but what do we do now, Fritz? We need to think clearly about what options are open to us; we need to weigh everything up against all the possible repercussions for us both although it will be assumed that we have both been killed during the today's action. They cannot charge a dead soldier with desertion'

'Our captain told us,' Fred continued, 'that if we reached and took what he called the H Line, which he said was built around a canal, then you Germans would surrender and this war would be over.'

'That's just about the same story we were told,' Fritz responded. 'But we were informed that if we let you Tommys breach our defensive lines we would all be killed, our throats would be cut and left to bleed to death. I knew that it was false but I didn't dare hint that our enemy had moral standards and would probably be sympathetic.'

'So, should I walk towards the British lines with you behind and your gun on me at all times?' Fritz suggested. 'I'll be your prisoner and you can inform your officers that I could be useful as an interpreter.'

'I'm not too sure about that,' Fred replied. 'Some of the lads have lost brothers and friends and they believe that there is no such thing as a good German. We can't take risks that will compromise our safety. If the war isn't over by now, then it soon will be. I suggest that we walk in the general direction of the canal, heading for St Quentin. By the time we get there the war may be over and the killing might have ended.'

The two soldiers, now showing a bit of trust in each other, set off at dawn, following what they believed to be the road to freedom, in the hope that the war was all but over. Neither soldier ever thought the word 'desertion' might be applied to their actions. After all, they had both done more than their bit for their country during this conflict.

The noise of the battle became fainter as they journeyed south and they only stopped to take rations and water from some of the poor men who had fallen during the fight. Fred ate dried biscuits and Fritz found some spicy sausage in a dead German soldier's backpack. He invited Fred to eat some, which he did, but Fred found it a bit difficult to digest. Both, however, felt uncomfortable stealing from their dead colleagues. Passing the scene of an intense battle and a totally destroyed German machine gun post, Fritz came across one poor soldier whose face, badly damaged from gunfire, was being made much worse by the rats and birds feeding off it. The rest of the body was not disfigured and the uniform was in good condition. Fred looked at Fritz. 'I hate to say this but why not take this soldier's uniform and identity papers. Then you can pass yourself off as this poor sod, if and when we come into contact with anyone in authority.'

Reluctantly, Fritz agreed and the two, respectfully, took all the clothes off the man before partially burying him to protect the corpse from rodents and further disfigurement

They both said a prayer over the body and Fred promised the dead man that he would return the private papers to his family whenever he could and wherever they may be.

Fritz took the uniform and identity of Jack Jackson, sergeant, 2nd Battalion, Canterbury Infantry Regiment (2/CIR) New Zealand Expeditionary Force (NZEF).

CHAPTER 06:
SERGEANT JACK JACKSON (NZEF)

Jack Jackson, twenty-eight years old, had been born on New Zealand's South Island in 1890. According to his papers he had been employed as a manager on a dairy farm in the Canterbury area and his letters revealed that he was married to Edna and had two children, a boy aged six and a girl aged four. The letters contained personal details of how much these two people loved each other and how the children missed their daddy. There was a photograph of his wife and the two children with a note on the back saying: 'Keep safe and return to us.' Fritz had to remember every detail in the event of being questioned.

The dead soldiers' undergarments were washed in a nearby stream and left out to dry in the mid-morning sun. Fritz put on the damp garments and both he and Fred walked away from the faint sound of gunfire, confident that they could carry out the deception if need be. Fred kept his rifle at the ready in case of any threats. Fritz took a rifle from the nearby dead soldier but Fred took the bullets out just in case his German friend changed his mind and wanted to return to his own lines.

Jack Jackson had lost his life during an act of extreme bravery, an act he embarked on with little concern for his own safety.

As the onslaught of German lines commenced in the NZ sector, the Allied soldiers moved forward, only to be caught in a hail of machine gun fire. Decisions had to be taken quickly in order to eliminate the cause of the growing number of casualties.

Sergeant Jack Jackson from Canterbury was given the task of planning an attack on a machine gun post located at the southern sector of the attack on German lines. This was classed as a very risky advancement and the captain in charge asked for six men who had experience of close, man-to-man fighting, in order to nullify this gun post. Five members of New Zealand's Canterbury Division stepped forward together with Lance Corporal George Mills, recently posted from the Duke of Cornwall's Light Infantry to give support and experience to new recruits to the battlefield.

The experienced sergeant gathered his team together. 'Right, lads, you know what you are up against. We could all be wiped out within minutes. In the event of a tragic ending we need to quickly write a few words for loved ones back home then let's be off and sort out these murdering swine.'

Sergeant Jackson hurriedly made a plan of attack. 'Two of you lads go forward to the left,' he directed, 'and two of you to the right. Keep your heads down as myself and George go up the centre line and draw the fire as you try to get behind the guns.' After agreeing the move forward, the sergeant spoke what he thought were some words of encouragement: 'We few, we happy few, we band of brothers. For he today who sheds blood with me shall be my brother. From today till the end of the world, this day shall be remembered and those who fought on this day, their names shall be spoken with pride and envy by they that did not fight and die alongside us gallant men.'

One member of the team who was getting ready for this difficult action said to the lance corporal: 'What a load of bollocks, where did he get that from? A kids' comic?'

The sergeant, who overheard the comment, shook his head and said nothing.

As Sergeant Jackson and Lance Corporal Mills moved up the hill from their previously hidden position, a hail of bullets came towards them. Luckily, what tree stumps were left gave them some cover but the machine gun unit, on realising this, shifted their attention to the tree stumps, leaving no place to hide. As arranged, the two from the left and the two from the right opened fire. This confused the Germans, leaving them unsure as to which way to shoot first. They quickly opened fire, one gun to the left and one gun to the right. This gave the opportunity for Jack and George to move forward each with a hand grenade ready to prime and throw into the nest. While the machine guns were engaged to both left and right the observer attached to the two guns saw that grenades were about to be thrown by the two soldiers.

Pistol in hand he had a split second; he had to choose one or the other. He would not survive the blast whatever option he chose, but he could possibly save the lives of the other two gunners. The taller of the attackers would probably throw the farthest so he made the decision to shoot him, which he did just before the grenade he threw landed in the dugout.

As it turned out, both grenades landed in the dugout, one at the front, one at the back and all three Germans were taken out, causing bits and pieces of bodies and uniforms to be scattered around the dugout. The sound of the explosion would no doubt attract the attention of any Germans in the vicinity and the decision was made by the lance corporal to leave the area and consolidate with the other forces and advance towards the German lines.

The relative success of the team of six was soured by the loss of their leader but they all praised the bravery of each other, particularly that of Jack, the sergeant in charge.

Reaching the main body of troops, the lance corporal reported the action of the day to his superiors and put great emphasis on the action and bravery of Sergeant Jackson. The officer in charge stated that he would personally make a report and recommend that some recognition be made to all six members of the attack unit that made such a significant contribution to the success of the day's actions.

CHAPTER 07:
RESCUE FROM THE ARGONNE FOREST

Fred and Fritz discussed what actions they should take and the immediate decision was to walk towards St Quentin and to take stock of the state of the war. Hopefully, the conflict would be over by the end of the day. If spotted by any authority they would explain that they were looking for one of the Allied units so they could join and get back in to the action.

They dreamed up a story of being captured by German forces from which they had escaped but, not knowing the geography of the area, they had become disorientated. They would explain how glad they were to meet up with another unit so that they could continue to fight. But, in reality, their thoughts centred on the fact that the war must be over and so they would not be at risk anymore.

Picking up some news regarding the state of the war, Fritz realised that the German army must have decided to carry on the fight in expectation of a miracle; a hope that they might turn the war back in their favour as had been the hope early on in 1918, when the Germans envisaged being in Paris within weeks. The appearance of the American forces, however, had the effect of changing the course of the war back in favour of the British and Allied forces.

Fritz suggested that they should consider heading towards the Alsace area of France, a region he was familiar with, hoping that they could find some transport to head towards the eastern part of the country.

After two days of walking and having hitched a ride on a farm truck, they were well south of St Quentin. Sitting on a wall, watching the world go by, they discussed their next move. Their thoughts were interrupted when a unit of young conscripted troops came by who had travelled from the Normandy area, heading towards the Argonne/Verdun region where they would be joining forces with French and American units tasked with pushing the German army back towards their homeland. Fred and 'Jack' reported to the officer in charge of what initially looked like a youth club weekend away. The officer looked more like a schoolboy than a leader of 200 soldiers. The two experienced soldiers offered to accompany the raw recruits as they convinced him that they were heading in the same direction. The officer gratefully accepted the offer of experience and invited them to join his unit and suggested that they perhaps gave his troops some training in 'close and intense fighting'. It soon became apparent that the recruits had been given the minimum training in the art of warfare and were in grave danger of becoming cannon-fodder as soon as they joined the front line. Travelling by whatever means of transport became available, it took another two days to reach the crossroads between the road coming south of Reims and the road travelling east towards Verdun.

On reaching Reims, Fred and 'Jack' had been instructed by the captain to follow him as they were to report to the senior officer who was situated in the Hotel Grand, a requisitioned hotel in the centre of what was left of a town that had seen some severe and concentrated fighting. The captain was to hand over his 200 charges so they could be allocated to whatever units were most in need. The captain added that he had two experienced British soldiers with him who had been on their way to Alsace Lorraine. He was ordered to bring the two soldiers to the hotel headquarters that was acting as the control sector for delivering troops to fight in the hills above Verdun.

The two soldiers were escorted to the hotel and had to sit in a dirty but pleasant waiting area until called forward and ushered into a room on the first floor, which had probably been a lounge area in the days when the building had operated as a hotel. A stern faced, elderly officer asked them to sit down before proceeding to scrutinise both Fred and 'Jack'. He was assisted by a small, plump man who appeared to be his secretary. He opened the meeting by asking questions of the soldiers in his basic English.

'Who are you?' the assistant asked

'Fred Mills, private, Duke of Cornwall's Light Infantry 30103,' Fred replied.

'Jack Jackson, sergeant, NZEF Canterbury Light Infantry 7206.'

Fritz identified himself as the name and rank of the soldier whose uniform he was wearing.

'Why are you so far away from the British sector?'

Both soldiers gave a pre-rehearsed explanation of events during the last days of September when they, and several other comrades, were confronted by a large group of deserting Germans and were forced to march with them towards the German border away from the areas of fighting. There were six of them and they'd planned to escape as soon the opportunity arose. During the second night of captivity the six made a run for it, just before dawn, when their guards were getting tired and attention was low. The Germans, however, quickly realised what had happened and gave chase to the escapees within twenty minutes of the escape. During captivity they had been given little food and all six were weak from exhaustion having previously fought for twelve hours without rest. The six became four as two soldiers changed direction and the four soon became two not long after. They'd heard shots in the distance and feared the worst for their colleagues. They continued the journey hoping to find some army unit with whom they could join up with and that is how they came to meet the unit from Normandy. Fred explained the events and the plump man translated as best he could. The two French interviewers discussed the merits of the explanation and 'Jack' listened intently as they commented positively on the story presented to them. The officer, through the translator, asked of their experiences of fighting. Both men had over two years' experience of fighting in the Somme area and had received commendations for bravery in hand-to-hand fighting, having been sent on a mission to capture a German officer in opposing trenches and bring him back for interrogation. The French officer was impressed with the story put forward and commented to his assistant that these two would be ideal to help with the situation in the Argonne Forest where 500 American soldiers were surrounded by a significantly larger German force.

The Argonne Forest had been in German control from the early days of the war. Since the beginning of September, the French, and latterly the Americans, had been gaining ground against the German defenders but further advancement was proving difficult. Fighting had become more intense in the hilly, forested terrain and the Germans held the superior position on the hills with snipers having significant success from well-hidden dens, instilling fear into the minds of the attacking forces.

The German defence lines were well constructed with sophisticated trench systems with tall barbed-wire obstacles covering all the defensive areas including the rivers and streams. This had made the area impossible to penetrate and thwarted the attempts of the Allied forces to gain control and rescue the captives held by the Germans who had no intention of giving up this part of eastern France. A strike force of 500 American troops had pushed forward towards the German defences, initially with some success. Unfortunately, the expected backup on either flank by French soldiers had not materialised and the American troops had become isolated, eventually finding themselves surrounded by German forces. The French and American forces that had successfully driven the Germans out of the villages were located in the heights above Verdun and had been unable to relieve those encircled by the German army.

After two days in the forest the Americans had suffered significant fatalities; many were injured while a number of soldiers had also been captured and interrogated. This allowed the Germans to gain a better knowledge of the Allied strength. The remaining American soldiers had run out of food and water as volunteers, who had attempted to get through enemy lines, had not been successful in reaching them. Two young soldiers had been caught and executed in full view of the American officers who witnessed the event through their high-powered binoculars. This had further weakened morale amongst the encircled troops. The officers in charge had been given the instruction 'not one step backward' and this had been carried out to the letter.

If these captives were to be killed by the German forces it would have a seriously demoralising effect, particularly on the insufficiently trained US troops. This would be seen as bad news back home and further evidence for not being involved in this war, especially as a large portion of the population in the United States had little or no concern for the ex-immigrant population whose roots lay in German-speaking countries. Nor was there much sympathy for those Scandinavians whose allegiance, for whatever reason, lay with Germany. In addition, memories of the loss of life during the American Civil War still left a bitter taste in the mouths of senior influential politicians who wanted their boys back home.

This was the situation put before Fred and 'Jack' who had little choice but to show enthusiasm at the chance to use their experience to help rescue the remaining soldiers trapped in the pocket.

The party of ten experienced soldiers tasked with rescuing the trapped US troops was assembled together to discuss rescue mission tactics. The eight French soldiers were suspicious of the two Tommys until 'Jack', in very broken French, did his best to explain the circumstances surrounding them being in the Meuse Argonne area. All seemed amicable until one of the French soldiers asked in English about where 'Jack' had learnt his broken French.

'I was educated in Canterbury, New Zealand,' 'Jack' replied, 'and our French speaking neighbours had a daughter just a couple of years older than me. We became secret friends and she taught me some basic French language amongst other things.' The inquisitive soldiers roared with laughter as he explained the story of the French man's daughter.

After the initial interrogation all became friends and, in the following days, they formed a close unit. Instructed by General Johnson, the senior officer in charge of the sector, and with the participation of all the men directly involved, a plan was agreed. Initially the mission involved five teams, each having two experienced volunteers who would take different routes into enemy territory.

Approximately half a mile was to be kept between the teams, some staying hidden for a period to allow a chosen pair to reach their objective. At a pre-arranged time, which would be decided on at the last minute, each team would open fire on a German position hoping to confuse the defenders and cause panic.

At the same time as shells were dropping into the eastern end of the pocket, the teams would rescue as many of the trapped soldiers as they were able and return to base. A larger force would then move forward a short distance away from the route planned for the escapees. The advanced troops would be tasked with entering the encircled area to drive the Germans back, allowing the escapees safe passage to American lines.

One team would be transported into the eastern sector, where it was suspected most of the prisoners were kept. The timing of their action would be discretionary depending on the circumstances and what options presented themselves. The captive soldiers would be in a poor state so great care needed to be taken if they were to make it out alive.

Because they spoke English, the two British soldiers were chosen to take on this task.

As the mission got under way, there was to be selective bombing of the northern part of the sector in the hope that the Germans would then expect them to attack that area; something that would not be taking place.

Having combat experience, both Fred and 'Jack' knew the philosophy of attack and defence strategies of both sides. The overall plan, as presented to them, seemed overcomplicated and carried too many risks. They were particularly concerned about the 'friendly fire' that was to take place with both the shelling then the exiting of the pocket. The French rescue soldiers had the benefit of knowing the area but had a disadvantage in that they did not speak English very well. Fred thought that if the American captives, who were so used to hearing English voices, heard French being spoken then they might be thrown into confusion: all foreign languages sounded the same to the average American from the Bronx. Such confusion might result in the captive American forces panicking and shooting anything that moved.

As the deadline for the action approached, an officer asked the two men if they wanted to write a letter to their loved ones back home, just in case they did not make it back alive. Both Fred and 'Jack' accepted that they might not survive this mission. An American officer came to discuss the final details and casually asked why the two British were not writing letters. Fred explained that they were satisfied for their families to be informed that they had been killed in action.

He and 'Jack' took the view that, if they got killed the next day fighting the Germans then they would prefer for their families to believe that they had been killed with the soldiers they had served with for the last two years and expressed their hope that the American officer could understand that.

Fred and 'Jack' walked 5 miles to the position indicated on the map that had been given to them by the captain co-ordinating the rescue mission. After a brief rest, the pair entered the enemy pocket through some dense undergrowth that both slowed the action but also had the advantage of giving cover as they advanced to the foot of what was shown on the map as Hill 72.

From a vantage point 'Jack' observed the location of the makeshift prison compound. 'Jack' led the way until they came to a barbed-wire obstacle. They had no hope of getting through but to the north of the compound there was a well-guarded gatehouse that allowed transport in and out. 'Jack' determined that the only way in was to go through this gate, create a diversion, take some senior officers hostage, free the prisoners located at this point, then get a truck and drive the prisoners out. It was as simple as that, but how, when and where could they execute this audacious rescue plan?

They spent the next hours observing activity through the gatehouse. As soon as night came it was noticed that some of the soldiers exited through the gate and headed towards a hiding place where it became obvious that some clandestine meeting had been arranged. In the distance a horse and cart could be seen and on the flat bed of that cart were two girls. It dawned on 'Jack' that these two were being used to entertain the two German soldiers. On closer inspection, one of the soldiers was dressed in an officer's uniform, which 'Jack' recognised by his insignia as Hauptmann, the same rank as captain.

It was clear that the soldiers on the gate had knowledge of this event and undoubtedly took turns to be with the 'captain'. After observing the movements of the German soldiers, a plan was agreed between the two rescuers. They would wait until the two Germans took their clothes off, attack them, kill the soldier then get the 'captain' to escort one of them through the gatehouse. Unfortunately, they would have to kill the girls in order to silence them, but, this was war and they couldn't see the women as anything other than traitors who deserved little pity.

The plan was carried out under the cover of darkness. The girls were killed first and then the soldier was despatched while still trying to pull up his trousers. The captain was too shocked to resist and, besides, was deeply embarrassed at being discovered with his trousers down. 'Jack', speaking German, took over and informed the 'captain' that he was from a special unit and needed to take the prisoners to a special location for an exchange which involved a high ranked officer, a member of the kaiser's extended family, who had to be rescued at all costs.

The captain did not believe a word of the story. The dialogue between 'Jack' and himself cast nothing but doubts and confusion in his mind but, if he hoped to survive this evening at all, then he was in no position to do anything else but co-operate.

'Jack', wearing the jacket and helmet belonging to the dead soldier, walked casually through the gate house with the 'captain'. It was pitch black and no suspicions were raised.

As if by a miracle, the northern sector came under heavy bombardment, causing immediate panic, leading German soldiers to believe that the Americans had actually commenced a rescue action to the north of the area they commanded. Fred was under instruction from 'Jack' to wait and observe the action. If the rescue mission had any degree of success then Fred should return back to base and inform the control centre that there would be a group of rescued soldiers being transported in a German truck, and not to fire on it.

The Hauptmann asked 'Jack' if he fully co-operated with all aspects of the mission would he be treated as a prisoner of war under the Geneva Convention. 'Jack' told him that, as far as he was able, he would protect him, particularly from the rescued men who would be angry at their maltreatment and would be seeking revenge. The Hauptmann took control of the situation and led 'Jack' to the prisoners area which had been partially destroyed by the bombing, leaving many German soldiers dead and injured.

Taking advantage of the confusion the Hauptmann ordered one of his subordinates to get a large truck ready to re-locate as many of the prisoners as possible as they had to be taken to another location to be used as part of a trade off towards negotiating an armistice to end the war.

The Hauptmann ordered two of his men to sit in the back of the truck and guard the rescued Americans, so adding credibility to the escape if stopped and questioned by German soldiers. After leaving the German sector by an indirect route, in order to allow time for Fred to get back to the control centre, the two soldiers were ordered by the Hauptmann to surrender their rifles as they were now prisoners of war and would be protected by both himself and the other soldier, 'Jack'. Both the war-weary German soldiers co-operated and the truck was greeted with cheers as they reached base.

After some close encounters, Fred made it back to the camp and gave the captain in charge all the details surrounding the actions that had been taken without giving away 'Jack's 'native' German language skills.

'Jack' informed the captain of the role played by the German officer and of the lack of resistance from the two German soldiers. 'Jack' told his captain, that each of these three Germans had officially surrendered to him on the understanding they would be treated as prisoners of war under the Geneva Convention and that, in the light of what has been achieved, this should be honoured. 'Jack' got an opportunity to speak privately to the Hauptmann, informing him of his German name, rank and number. In return the German officer gave 'Jack' his own details.

Speaking quietly, in German, 'Jack' told his prisoner not to ask any questions or to give away any details regarding their discussion.

'Remember,' 'Jack' said, 'I have saved your life and rescued you from what is about to become a total onslaught on the German defences, one that you would not have survived. We will meet again in better circumstances, but what has gone on between us must not be divulged as it could be critical to the German nation after this war has ended.'

Having exchanged details, 'Jack' called the guard over and left the Hauptmann to be arrested and interviewed alongside the two soldiers.

The other pairs of rescuers had had mixed success with only three of the pairs returning with captives, while 'Jack' had returned with twenty-eight rescued soldiers, although eight of them were in a poor state of health. The rescued soldiers were given water then immediately taken to a hospitalised unit that had been prepared for them after the rescue had been successfully achieved. The following day an influx of America soldiers arrived from St Nazaire to cover for the losses that had occurred.

They had suffered an horrendous crossing of the Atlantic, leaving the whole contingent of men, and a few women nurses, in a permanent state of sea-sickness. The rough seas had, however, curbed attacks from the German submarine packs that covered vast swathes of the Atlantic.

In the days and weeks that followed, the superior number of

American combatants, coupled with the total breakdown of morale, had resulted in the German army retreating to their rear defence lines where they waited for the expected onslaught by the fresher American forces.

Fred and 'Jack' were treated as heroes and, after two days recuperation, were taken to the headquarters of the American command to debrief with General Johnson, commander in charge of the Argonne offensive.

Talk of citations were played down by the two soldiers as they told the general that they were just part of a team who had happened to have fortune on their side and that they should not be treated any differently from other soldiers who had taken part in the mission. Some had been successful, while others had lost their lives trying to rescue American forces. They put forward the case that it should be the whole unit who receive awards, citation and medals, certainly not individual soldiers.

The general admired their stance but explained that he could not recommend awards to the group as a whole unit, as medals were for individual feats of bravery not group actions. The general gave Fred and 'Jack' a letter each outlining the actions they had taken to rescue the trapped soldiers along with his personal card inscribed with his name and details suggesting that they arrange to meet with him after the war in order to reconsider what they had discussed. He gave orders for each of them to return to the rear lines where, after a brief period of leave, they were to be allocated to a special unit where they would train suitable soldiers by sharing their own field experience, especially concerning undercover observation techniques and survival training. They would be staying in a chateau commissioned by the Americans and put at their disposal until the end of the war, which the general believed would be within the next few days.

Before leaving his office, General Johnson looked coolly at the two soldiers and asked how they had managed to convince this Hauptmann to co-operate with them when the man didn't speak a word of English.

The general continued his questioning, his voice inquisitive: 'I just don't understand how you managed to carry out the mission so successfully. Is there something you are not telling me?'

'No, sir,' answered Fred. 'We just had opportunity, good luck and a war weary, co-operative German officer.'

'Bullshit,' replied the general. 'We will meet up after the war and fill in the missing details. By the way, before you do anything else, please change out of those stinking uniforms. Go to the quartermaster's stores and get kitted out in number twos.'

With that, they left the office and proceeded to take up their new orders travelling back down the line and taking transport to Reims to a confiscated large house just outside the centre of town. On arrival, they were shown their room and given a programme of training responsibilities that, actually, left a fair amount of spare time to explore the city of Reims: perhaps even to try a glass or two of the local brew: Champagne.

CHAPTER 08:

DELIVERING BAD NEWS

The same day that Fred was meeting with General Johnson, his younger brother, Harold, spotted the postman walking down from Queens Street to the entrance of Kempsey Street.

The postman dreaded this part of his job: bringing bad news from the front.

'Go get your mother, Harold,' the postman ordered, 'and tell her to sit down.'

Mary Anne had been hanging the washing out on the line and was busy talking to Alice, her sister-in-law, who lived next door. They kept each other up to date with the local news, particularly anything to do with the war.

'Our George wrote to us yesterday,' Alice told her friend, 'and he said that all was quiet on the western front, but a big push forward was anticipated soon. He said in his letter that your Fred had teamed up with some lads from New Zealand and that he was going to emigrate once the war was over to start a new life in a new country, away from all the death and carnage he had been living with.'

'Well, I've not heard from him since the beginning of September,' Mary Anne replied, 'and he said nothing then about New Zealand, Timbuktu or anywhere else for that matter other than Oldham.'

When Harold shouted for his mother to come to the front door a shiver went through her.

'Sit down, Mary Anne,' the postman said gently. 'It looks like bad news, I'm so sorry.'

Mary Anne collapsed and if not for the swift reactions of Harold and the postman, her head would have crashed onto the stone floor. Harold tried to comfort his mother but she was inconsolable after being told that her eldest boy had been lost.

'Get off to work, Harold,' she cried, 'and ask the over-looker in the ring room to allow our Eddie to leave work early. Tell the boss that your mother has had some bad news.'

Edward was Mary Anne's third son after Fred and William and just twelve months older than Harold. Eddie was temporarily filling in at work for one of the ring spinners who had lost the tip of his index finger by getting his sleeve caught in the gearing at the rear of the machine he was attending to. Eddie, at just seventeen, had been called up for a non-combat role in a relief station where he would be trained as a hospital orderly whose job it would be to keep the surgical area clean and tidy.

After informing both the over-looker and Eddie, Harold sat in a corner thinking tearfully about how much he loved and would miss his elder brother. His other brother, William, who was three years older than Harold, had physical issues that he kept to himself and told people that he wasn't allowed to go to fight due to his job as a Turner/Miller in the machine shop at Platt's factory in Werneth. He had become a very skilled and productive worker and the management had explained to the army recruitment people that William was essential to the war effort.

Because of his importance to the company, William was given a room on site where he was expected to keep an eye on the efficiency of the machines in his section, which meant him having periods of interrupted sleep as he showed his face to the lads on the night shift in order to maintain the levels of production and even improve upon the standard and output that he had promised the section manager. He was favoured by one of the Platt family's cooks who made him his meals and occasionally tucked him up in bed with a goodnight kiss.

Harold was left at home with his two sisters, Dolly and May, and his younger brother George. He was a shy lad, but his handsome good looks made him a target of attention from some of the girls who worked in the ring room.

The three Riley sisters: Martha, Lizzie and Bertha were fond of Harold and the two elder sisters would say things to him that would make him blush. The youngest sister, Bertha, had promised Harold her first kiss when she was eighteen

The Riley girls' father, Joe, had been requisitioned by the army to undertake secret work in Flanders and Northern France. He did not disclose the nature of his duties, even to his wife, Sarah, but his job as a gravedigger at Hollinwood Cemetery had narrowed down what his duties might be.

Digging up dead bodies was the last job that Joe would have wanted, but he was keen to do his duty, especially for the young lads who had fallen like pawns in a game dictated by faceless men in Whitehall.

CHAPTER 09:
BURIAL RETRIEVAL UNIT (BRU)

Joe Riley belonged to what was called the Burial Retrieval Unit (BRU). The job of the BRU was to recover bodies of fallen soldiers and take one of their identity disks for identification. A record was taken as to the location of the body, leaving the other disk on the body. The body of the fallen soldier would then be taken to a predetermined burial area well behind the forward lines where a formal burial service could be carried out. One cynical Tommy was heard to say that you got treated better once you were dead than you did when you were alive.

The unit usually consisted of a team of five or six men. It had been decided, by the upper echelons of the army, that it would have a negative effect on soldiers marching to the front to have to get involved or see the results of death on the battlefield, so Joe's unit tended to stay remote and keep themselves to themselves.

It had been Joe's first trip to a foreign country and his first time away from home in Oldham: apart from a charabanc trip to Blackpool, where he had played the euphonium with the Hollinwood and District Brass Band in the Tower Ballroom. His only other experience of a foreign land was his birth in Pontiac, Rhode Island to

Isaac Riley and Martha Fletcher, who had left the port of Liverpool to lead a new life in the promised land of America.

Both his parents had been attracted by an advertisement in the Manchester Evening News that promised a new and better life working at Knights Mill in Pontiac about five miles from Providence, the capital of the state of Rhode Island. Both Isaac and Martha were single and had no ties back in Oldham. The United States of America had just come through the devastation of the American Civil War, fought between the Union Northern States who opposed slavery and the Confederate Southern States who saw slavery as essential. In the South, slaves were used to pick cotton and tobacco crops in order to maintain and even add to the extravagant lifestyles of the owners, a lifestyle gained through the exploitation of black people who had been forcibly taken from their families in Africa.

The war between 'brothers' ended in 1865, which triggered the start of a boom in demand for goods of any description. With this boom came a need for skilled labour. America, once behind Europe in technology development, soon caught up, then overtook the home of the industrial revolution by using the very labour that had been responsible for Europe's industrial development.

Martha and Isaac were both skilled textile workers. In spite of having lived within three miles of each other, they had never met before sailing to Boston from Liverpool in the fourth-class steerage section of the boat, 'generously' paid for by the Knight brothers, Robert and Benjamin, owners of Pontiac Mills. The entrepreneur's booming business was the manufacture of cotton goods under the logo: 'Fruit of the Loom'.

The voyage across the Atlantic was mostly calm. That was until a sudden squall severely rocked the boat and the previously separated men and women were ordered to assemble in the main dining hall where the women were issued with life jackets. Fourth-class men were not issued with any life jackets: perhaps they were expected to swim the freezing thousand miles or so to the shores of the USA.

A sudden lurch threw everyone together and it was fortunate that Isaac managed to catch Martha before her head cracked against the steel column in the centre of the room.

'Are you with someone?' Isaac asked as the ship steadied.

'I'm just a single girl from Ashton,' Martha replied. 'What about you, are you with someone? Perhaps we could meet when the boat docks.' Martha suggested, taking the lead with a shy Isaac. A voice from the control room made an announcement requesting that everyone go back to their quarters and that was the last they saw of each other on the boat. They docked in Boston, then everyone was transported the forty-five miles to Providence.

It was some weeks after their arrival that Isaac and Martha met again, and, as they quickly became infatuated with each other, fellow workers suggested that they should get married as soon as possible. Both attended church back home and they took great pleasure in meeting after church on Sundays.

The Pontiac Company had plans to build a new church in the grounds owned by the Knight brothers, but in the meantime services were held in the Mill canteen. So, it was in the canteen cum All Saints Rectory that Isaac and Martha were married on 24th of April 1871 and it was just over nine months later that John Joseph Riley was born to the couple.

Joe knew the story of his parent's emigration to the United States but the reason for their return to England was never explained or discussed. Joe assumed that it must have been something serious for them to leave the 'promised land' and return to Oldham.

As Joe got older he became proud of his history and, at the age of eleven, he told his best friend, Stephen, the story of his parent's time in America: the land where he was born. But Joe regretted boasting about his American identity when he became the subject of torment from some of the lads at school who started calling him Yankee Doddle Do and other such derisory names. Standing his corner got Joe into fights: some he won, some he didn't, but it was after one particular fight when he bloodied the nose of Jimmy Quinn, the cock of the school, that Joe became respected and befriended by the other lads.

The sister of one of his friends took a shine to Joe, and at the age of twenty-one, Joe and Sarah Leach became man and wife. They suffered the terrible disappointment of losing their first-born twins but the couple went on to have three girls: Martha, Elizabeth and Bertha.

Joe's secret trip to France had given him a unique perspective on the terrible carnage that the war had inflicted on brave young men from both sides of the battle. He had picked up scattered bodies of many young men, some of whom were just children that had got caught up in a senseless war.

On the 27 September 1918 Joe had been put in charge of a group of men asked to ready themselves for a major push forward into enemy lines. What they were really being told was to prepare themselves because there were going to be a lot of bodies to bury.

The attack on the German lines was planned to commence on the 29 September and the intensity of the advancement would result in the BRU teams readying themselves for a huge amount of work.

The focal point of any battle always saw the greatest losses and it took four days for a team to reach the slightly isolated battle area that had been involved in an attack to take out a machine gun position. The Allies had pushed the enemy back and Joe's team were able to assess the damage inflicted in the previous three days. They went up an incline where they saw bits of dead Germans spread over a 10 yard radius, the result of hand grenades being thrown into their position.

The machine gun had certainly done its damage before it was taken out, with most bodies being at the bottom of the rise. Experience indicated to Joe that a fierce battle had taken place. As Joe was assessing the amount of equipment needed to clear the site, his eye was caught by what looked to be a half buried body part way up the rise of the land. The dead man's face had been half eaten by vermin and he appeared to be without his uniform jacket.

Joe shouted his team to come down the hill. 'Come and look at this. Poor fellow has lost his top tunic. Let's get him uncovered and wrapped up.'

As Joe and a fellow helper pulled the body out, Joe exclaimed, 'Bloody hell, someone's pinched all his clobber and left him starkers. Never seen that before. Young Jimmy, run and get that bald sergeant. Get him over here to see this.'

After assessing what sort battle had taken place, writing notes about the location, the probable action and details of this naked body, the sergeant ordered that it be taken separately into Perone.

The sergeant told Joe: 'I'm going to request an investigation into what could have happened to this poor lad. I have never come across anything like it in the whole of my career and believe me, I have seen some sights in my time.'

THE END OF THE WAR

11 o'clock on the 11th day of the 11th month.
   After four years, three months and two weeks of conflict.
   After the death of at least 8,573,054 military personnel.
   After the death of at least 7,661,099 civilians.
   After a global conflict involving thirty-two countries.
   The aggressors finally admitted defeat and an armistice was signed at 5.45 am on the morning of 11 November 1918 in the Railway Carriage of Marshall Foch located in Compiegne.
   This armistice was to come into force at 11.00 am that same morning
   It was a great pity that no one told the killer of George Edwin Ellison of the 5th Royal Irish Lancers; killed while out scouting at 9.30 am that same morning.
   But perhaps the greatest shame was the German sniper who shot and killed Private George Lawrence Price at 10.58, two minutes before the Armistice.
   The end of war document contained thirty-four clauses concerning the cessation of all activities, the treatment of sick and wounded, the evacuation of land, the giving up of all types of materials and the release of prisoners of war. On top of that, there

were some very detailed clauses regarding the compensation to be paid from the defeated to the victors.

All of it was to be wrapped up in the Treaty of Versailles.

Who won?

Nobody won!

Who lost?

Everybody lost.

But it was the war to end all wars!

Pity nobody told Lance Corporal Adolf Hitler of the List Regiment who was hospitalised at Pasewalk suffering from blindness due to a British mustard gas attack.

He had also lost his voice, and what a great shame for the entire world that he ever recovered it.

But that is another story!

CHAPTER 10:
CELEBRATIONS

In Reims there followed an exciting weekend of celebration with newly found American friends and friends of friends, who were only too keen to help these 'Doughboys' spend their money and share in the fun. People came from miles around to join in the fantastic atmosphere and as the evening drew on, the local police had to keep the crowds under some sort of control. The living were out celebrating and, just for a moment, the dead were forgotten. Some of the famous Champagne houses helped fuel the fun by opening their cellars, for a time, to anyone wearing a uniform and, with this celebratory drink flowing, the mood of the city was in total contrast to the previous four years of German occupation. But that was now history.

The conflict over the last two weeks of the war had become less intense but it had still been dangerous to be on the front trenches with soldiers still getting killed and injured. The volume of casualties in the hospitals and clearing stations had been reduced from its peak at the end of September through the first weeks of October: many of the injured being helped back to life by hard working and dedicated nurses. There were also society girl helpers, if helpers is the correct word for these ex-boarding school, free spirited females, all of whom wanted a piece of the action. Their main goal had not been to help with the victims of conflict, death and maiming but to experience freedom away from 'mummy' and 'daddy': to live it up before getting married off to some second son of a tenth generation aristocrat.

The American soldiers with their 'cute' accents got their share of this free spirit, but it was the boys from the Bronx and Harlem in New York who became the favourites of some of the more adventurous girls. Back home it was frowned on and in some southern states, it was even illegal for a black man to 'date' a white woman. But in Reims no such restrictions applied and the boys loved it.

The four weeks following the rescue of the American soldiers had been a bit of an ordeal for Fred and 'Jack'. With their fame came inevitable questions regarding the specifics of how they had carried off such a successful rescue mission. Fred and 'Jack' had become the centre of attention and, after the Armistice when units started to be dismissed, the city of Reims became a melting pot of all nationalities. Soldiers relieved from duty around the Somme area started to drift south and Fred and 'Jack' became concerned that they might get recognised by previous colleagues. The work they had undertaken, training recruits in concealment techniques, had run its course and on the 15 November the classes finished with the two heroes being given permission from senior officials to leave: they were free. They both had letters from General Johnson, which, after one week's notice, and on leaving the chateau, allowed them free travel.

'We need to leave soon,' Fred urged 'Jack'. Fred realised that the longer they stayed in Reims the more likely it would be for their identities to be compromised. Fred and 'Jack' had, during last week, become friendly with two trainee French nurses who had received permission to leave Reims and travel to their home in Gerardmer, in the Vosges mountain area. 'Jack' suggested that they leave with the girls and travel as far as they were going, perhaps staying around for a couple of weeks before deciding where to go next. 'Jack' was keen to get to the Alsace region so he could find a way of getting a message to his mother without his father knowing.

Uniforms had been replaced by civilian clothing with each of the men keeping the army jackets as a memento of the war experience and to also give proof of identity should it be required.

'Jack' carried the personal effects of the fallen soldier, which he would later pass on to Fred, who would keep his promise to inform the soldier's family as to the circumstances leading to him being in possession of their loved one's personal papers.

They wrote a letter for General Johnson to the effect that they had taken advantage of an opportunity to travel south with two nurses but thanked the general for giving them the opportunity to work in the chateau. The training that they had overseen had probably helped save many lives, not least the lives of raw recruits sent over from the United States with very little training.

By the time the letter appeared on the general's desk, the group of four were one hundred kilometres south and not too far from the girls home. The two men agreed that when the opportunity arose they would leave the girls. They had not taken any advantage of them and that evening after a night in a flea pit of a country lodging house which had probably been deserted until recently but re-occupied with a view to offering cheap accommodation to the thousands of soldiers returning to the various departments of France. Jack explained in his pretend broken French that he and Fred needed to leave to meet up with others in the Colmar area. The girls were disappointed because they had glimpsed a future with these two soldiers who had behaved like such gentlemen towards them. Fred and 'Jack' took their names and addresses and promised that if things did not work out in Colmar then they would get back in contact within three months.

Accepting a lift in a cattle wagon travelling to Colmar and passing within five kilometres of Nancy, the girls' home, they reached a crosswords where the four parted. It was an emotional departure with promises made from both sides. The wagon driver was keen to get on his way so with a last hug and kiss the boys were on the way again. They travelled another ten kilometres before the driver pulled into a village and offered the men a night's accommodation at his friend's home.

After an uncomfortable night sleeping in a barn, the two soldiers washed as best they could in cold water from a horse trough then set off to look for some hotel or lodging house in the next village: Flavigny on the Moselle.

CHAPTER 11:
YVETTE AND CELINE

On reaching the village of Flavigny, there was a rowdy atmosphere: a combination of freedom from the war and happy people joining friends for the village's market day. Fred and Fritz took seats at one of the bars in the market square and ordered two large glasses of local red wine. Several discussions were taking place around them and Fritz listened in, offering Fred the outline of what was being discussed. All the talk was about the war. The table next to theirs was reflecting on men who had returned or were due to return and of those who would never return. On another table, an elderly man held counsel stating that he had seen it all before after the German/Prussian Army had defeated the French and taken lands in Alsace. His view was to not only take these lands back, but to also take land from the east of the Rhine, both as punishment and to protect France from another German attack because, in his view, France would never be safe from their Teutonic neighbours. All agreed and discussions went on and on in the same vein. The discussion relating to German lands being given back to France made Fritz realise that this change of borders between France and Germany would have a direct effect on his father, who, although not interested in politics, was nevertheless staunchly German. Fritz decided that he had to, somehow, get a discreet message to his mother to let her know that he had survived the war and was, for the moment, staying in France.

A loud and aggressive argument between two women interrupted the joyful atmosphere of the bar. It appeared to 'Jack' that one of the women had travelled some distance and was accompanied by a man who was drinking large glasses of the local spirit and had fallen asleep at his table.

Fred asked 'Jack' what the two women were arguing about. It appeared that the elder of the two women had received news some weeks ago that her husband and brother-in-law had both been killed fighting in the Verdun area and that she had, in turn, written to inform the other woman who was the young sister of the fallen soldiers.

This younger woman lived somewhere in the south west of France, near the Spanish border, and, on receiving the sad news, had immediately travelled with her drunken male companion to claim the farm property owned by her brothers and to inform her brother's widow that she should arrange to leave the farm. The younger told the elder that the farm would be run by her and her new family who would bring it back into a fully functioning state.

This younger sister had secretly visited the farm early in the morning, before her sister-in-law had risen from her bed, and found the farm overgrown and in a very poor state of repair. The older woman, whose name was Yvette, explained to the younger woman, Celine, that she had no intention of leaving the farm and that she had a letter from her husband to the effect that if anything happened to him he would leave the farm to his wife and his brother. The fact that his brother had also been killed did slightly complicate matters, but she, Yvette, had possession and was not giving it up. Yvette explained that now the war was over she would have a much better chance of getting some male help on the farm, instead of some of the chancers whom she had employed previously. Some of these men, most of whom had been deemed unfit for whatever reason to fight for their country, had seen Yvette as an easy target being on her own, but when called upon, she had either fought them off herself or received assistance from a local farmer and his son.

As the argument continued, everyone's attention, which had previously been centred on enjoying a peaceful market day, was now focused on these the two women. It was only when the younger women struck the other on the face and drew blood that 'Jack' stepped forward to part them.

'Who do you think you are?' Celine challenged 'Jack'. 'This is none of your business and if you don't go away I will have to tell my friend, over there, to teach you better manners about not getting involved in other people's private business.' 'Jack' laughed at the thought of the drunken man being even able to stand up let alone being fit to fight anything or anyone.

'Actually, myself and my colleague here have just returned from the war and were about to offer our services as farm labourers to this lady who you are being so aggressive to.'

'You obviously do not know who you are dealing with here,' Celine replied. 'My husband is Jon the Basque from the area of Bayonne in the south west of France, better known as the Basque country. We are a very independent people and we would fight to the death to protect our lands, our culture, our people and, in this case, our property. So please, go and sit down with your friend and leave me to sort out my private matters without your, or anyone else's interference.'

After the younger woman and her half-drunk colleague had left the market square, 'Jack' approached the woman, Yvette: 'Apologies for the intrusion, but I couldn't help but hear that you and the other woman were having a very serious argument regarding your farm. My friend and I here have just left Reims where we have been fighting the Germans. If you are still looking for assistance in running your farm, then, perhaps we could help for a short period.'

Some of the local inhabitants were aware of the story about Celine. She had left the farm at the age of fifteen, just before the outbreak of the war, and had travelled with a close friend to work in one of the big hotels in Biarritz. It became the routine of the two girls to go to one of the bars along the jetty on their day off and mix with the locals who drank the local spirit and ate a selection of different kind of foods, freshly cooked, which the locals called tapas. The people there spoke in a language completely different to French and totally different to the Spanish dialect spoke just over the border in San Sebastian. Unknown to the girls, two of the local young men had been discussing the assets of the girls and one of the young men, whose name was Jon, was explaining to the other what he would like to do with the girl called Celine. On hearing her name being spoken, Celine turned to the young man, Jon, and smiled. She smiled not even knowing what he had said except she knew it was something sexual when the barman came over and chastised Jon, then apologised to Celine in French. Jon came over to Celine later and apologised for his rude behaviour. It was, he said, because he had been working in the fields and had had nothing to eat so the alcohol had taken over his tongue. Celine had replied that whatever he'd said she didn't mind and that she had guessed it had been something close and personal.

'Please let me escort you girls back to your lodgings,' said Jon. 'I believe that you are working in the Hotel du Palais. It is a beautiful hotel; full of rich people and some of the wealthy young men will be on the lookout for a good looking girlfriend to put on their arm for the duration of their stay, but these rich boys will love you and leave you. Please be careful, pretty girl.'

Celine was grateful for the advice and as they reached the hotel Jon kissed her hand, telling her that if she ever needed help to just 'go to the bar on the jetty and tell anyone there that you need some help from Jon the Basque.'

In fact, only days later at the end of that week, as she was cleaning one of the superior rooms overlooking the sea, the occupant, a famous politician from just north of Paris came back into the room, locked the door from the inside and started making indecent suggestions to Celine. Celine who was aware that this could happen knew she could not scream or shout for help: the advice given to any young girls who happened to be caught in an uncompromising situation was to tell the man that she was in the middle of her monthlies and would be available for some passion in two days.

A quick peck on the cheek and perhaps a squeeze of her breasts would take the sting out of him. If this occurred, she must tell the head housekeeper who, in conjunction with the manager, would either challenge the man discreetly, or, if he was a special guest, would move the girl away from cleaning the room and replace her with one of the older, plumper and less attractive members of staff.

Celine was very upset by this man's attitude towards her and decided to go to the jetty and tell Jon what had happened. Jon wasn't due to be in the bar until later so she passed the details of what had happened to one of the labourers in the kitchen who happened to be Jon's cousin.

Celine was upset when she met Jon sometime later and told him the story of what had happened. Jon told her not to worry, to carry on as if nothing had occurred and to please keep smiling so as not to look suspicious.

At some point, the politician received an urgent phone call, checked out early and nothing was heard of the man for many months until he was found dead in a remote part of Lombardy in northern Italy with his penis in his mouth. He had, according to the autopsy, choked to death on his member.

The news about finding the body and the circumstances of his death should have been front page news in the Paris Matin newspaper, but the events of the previous day in a city called Sarajevo and the response from the Austrians had resulted in the report of the dead French politician being placed in a small section of the sixth page!

As events unfolded following the assassination of Archduke Franz Ferdinand and his wife, Sophie, and as Germany subsequently invaded France, the prospect of Jon, his brothers, cousins and friends being called up to fight for France became a real possibility.

Jon was a Basque from the country Euskal. It was not recognised as a sovereign state but the occupants on both sides of the French/Spanish border knew the Euskal inhabitants were a distinct group of people who would defend their land to the death. They had no fight with Germany, Austria, Hungary or any of the allies of these countries: they would not fight for France or anyone else so arrangements had to be made to allow the young Basque men to find refuge over the border in Spain, out of the reach of French authority.

The Basque's had a love-hate relationship with both the French and Spanish police but, particularly on the French side, the local police would come into the Basque area for no other reason than to receive delicious food, fine wine and a brown envelope. This arrangement with the police had existed for many years and, when an army recruiting post was set up in Bayonne, there was little interest shown.

After the incident with the politician Jon and Celine became a couple. Celine left the hotel after the summer season, which had been disrupted by the impending war and went to stay with an aunt of Jon's to ensure that no intimacy occurred between them until the wedding, which was arranged for late in the autumn of 1914. Celine's family could not travel as the railways were being controlled by events in the north of France,

The wedding was an all Basque affair, and what a celebration it was! It was only after three days of food, drink and entertainment that the event actually ended and guests left to go back to their villages. The guest of honour, the chief of police for the department of Pyrenees-Atlantique, had never known such enjoyment in the whole of the sixty years he'd been alive.

CHAPTER 12:
FLAVIGNY

In the village of Flavigny, the heated discussion between ladies had petered out. Celine, took a bucket, filled it with water from a horse trough, threw in a shovel of manure then woke her drunken colleague by chucking the contents all over him. This rapidly brought the man to his senses and the two soon left with Celine telling her sister-in-law that she would back.

Yvette had been taken aback by the forthrightness of the man who had interrupted her discussions with Celine, telling him that he should not have been listening in to other people's conversations. Following the offer of work from the two strangers she had asked, 'I don't know who you are and why I should trust you above any of the cretins that have offered to work on my farm: men who never had any intention of working. They just wanted to take advantage of a woman whose husband was away fighting for our freedom.'

'Jack' could well understand the woman's concerns and offered for both himself and his friend to work on the farm for two or three days, without pay. After that, both parties could see if they got on together and if there could be some work for the two men over the winter period.

Having few alternatives, Yvette agreed to give the two soldiers a week's work on the farm. The work would be extremely hard as the fields had to be cleared of weeds, overgrown saplings that had taken root and other debris that had made the farm unproductive since her husband and his brother had left to fight for France.

'I will give you good food and there will be a barrel of ale for you to drink,' Yvette told them. 'But I have little money and cannot afford to give you any of my meagre savings.'

Both men agreed to the terms and formally introduced themselves as 'Jack' from New Zealand, nicknamed Fritz, and Fred from the north of England.

The farm was just over five kilometres from the village square. Yvette rode ahead in her horse and cart, the horse looking as though its days were numbered and the cart looking ready to fall to pieces at any time. Fred and 'Jack' followed some distance behind, discussing en route what might have happened with the woman Celine and her family. Both men knew that they would have to be vigilant and 'Jack' suggested that they had better get a rifle or gun as there was no doubt that the sister-in-law would return and that she would not be back on her own.

'There will be plenty of guns for sale,' 'Jack' reasoned. 'I will go back to Nancy and discreetly ask at the local Bar Tabac about what might be available.'

The following week on the farm was extremely hard work, but the two men grafted from dawn to dusk only stopping at noon to eat the best part of a loaf of bread each, accompanied by some very mature cheese and strong flavoured onions. In the evenings Yvette prepared a large pot of lamb stew, which she set up on an old oak table, probably handed down through many generations.

She left the men to eat and drink then retired to her room where she ate on her own, reminiscing about times spent with her husband before all the carnage began.

After the week of hard work ended, Yvette sat down for the evening meal and thanked the men for the graft that they had put in and apologised for not being able to reward them financially. The next day, on the way to the village, Yvette visited one of the farmers who had helped her while her husband and brother-in-law had been away fighting. Now that two of the fields were ready for planting she could offer one of the upper fields to the farmer in return for some financial help so she could plant crops in the lower fields. It had been the local farmer who had suggested such an arrangement should take place, if and when the war ended as there would be an increase in demand for the excellent fruit and vegetables the farm was famed for. That way both the farmer and Yvette would be better off.

Her visit proved successful and the local farmer provided seed, fertiliser and some farm implements, which would help Yvette's farm to begin to flourish after the winter period.

Yvette sat down with the two men and explained the arrangement she had made with the local farmer. She told them that this would allow her to pay them for working on both her field and on the field given to the local farmer.

'Jack', on his visit to Nancy, had successfully located an American sniper rifle with over one hundred bullets and informed Yvette that he would pick up the rifle the following Saturday.

During the evening meal Yvette relayed to the men the story about Celine. How they had lived together when she married her brother and how they have become like sisters. That relationship had changed when she married Jon and took on the culture and the nature of the clan she had married into.

'Very dangerous people,' Yvette explained. 'We need to be careful because they will return soon to try to take the farm from me. They will be delighted that the farm is about to go back into some level of production.'

Fred and 'Jack' discussed various options and one suggestion was that if Yvette helped 'Jack' in the fields, Fred could guard the farm in the periods that an attack was most likely.

'If they come, they will come at dawn,' Fred reasoned. 'I'll build a hideaway that will give me a full vista of the farm buildings so if there are intruders then I will have them in my sights and respond as necessary.' The plan of action was agreed and the rota of work, observation and sleep was carried out.

CHAPTER 13:

JON

When Celine returned from Flavigny, she explained to Jon what had happened after a meeting she had with her sister-in-law to discuss ownership of the farm. Jon was disappointed at the outcome but he would, when time allowed, visit the farm himself and do what was necessary to recover what rightly belonged to them.

Jon and his friends had previously fled the area of the Basque country that belonged to France in order to avoid being called up by the army: the group had no loyalty to France and had no reason to kill Germans. They had spent most of the four years in the Spanish Basque region hiding from Spanish authorities, who had been offered a financial incentive from the French police to round up these 'French' non-combatants and hand them over to police in Bayonne.

Fear of the Basque repercussions if they were seen to be helping the French police and authorities had resulted in the Spanish police turning a blind eye to most of the activities undertaken by Jon and his group. Consequently, Jon's Basque group had been free to roam over most of the south west of France and the adjoining Spanish lands.

The one exception to the indifference of the Spanish police was a sergeant in the border town of Irun. Michel Etxarri had a personal grievance against Jon after one of Jon's group had abused the sister of his friend. Michel, who had been in the Spanish police for over ten years, kept a close eye on Jon's activities and noticed how Jon and his friends crossed the border by the same mountain path every second Thursday, returning on the next day, Friday.

Michel would one day use this knowledge to his advantage.

In the spring following Celine and Yvette's disagreement, Jon had arranged for a posse of men to accompany him to help take control of his wife's farm. As was his routine, he crossed the French/Spanish border on a Thursday under the cover of a moonless night. The six men knew the way and walked confidently and silently over the well-defined track that was partially covered by trees and large cabbage like plants. The group felt confident that they were well hidden from view.

It came as a total surprise, therefore, when the group found themselves surrounded by a large number of armed French police aided by the Spanish sergeant.

The Basques were outnumbered. The police had the advantage having the element of surprise. The Basques became involved in a fight for their lives against well-armed forces with modern weapons. Jon's group were quickly and efficiently out-classed and four of the six were killed. With their superior numbers and the element of surprise, the police had not considered that they would be in any danger but one of the policemen, a recent recruit to the force, became isolated and was shot and killed during the action.

Jon survived the fight as it was the intention of the police not to kill him, but to arrest him, so he could be put on trial as an example to the men who lived on the French/Spanish border area: it would be a message to them that the French police had control of the area and would be carrying out routine actions to round up deserters who had avoided the call up to fight for the freedom of France against the German aggressors.

The two surviving Basque men were handcuffed and taken to the area police HQ in Bayonne. They would not stay there long as the police wanted to transport the captured men as quickly as possible to Paris. There they would be put on trial for the murder of a policeman.

Being found guilty, they would, without doubt, be hanged for their crimes and the police would then gain control of what they saw as part of France, not an independent country.

On the way to Paris the police had arranged for several changes of drivers and vehicles to reflect the distance between Bayonne and Paris. The first change was arranged to be just outside Bordeaux, eight hours from Bayonne. Food was to be brought for the prisoners and they would be allowed to relieve themselves while still handcuffed to one of the officers, who would be armed with a hand gun.

The exchange car was late and the driver and officer were tired from the journey. It was just before the driver exchange that Jon managed to loosen his handcuffs. When they stopped, he snatched the gun from the weary officer, killed both the officer and driver and released the handcuffs from both himself and his companion. The pair left the scene in the direction of the railway goods yard, hoping for a train travelling south west so they could return to their homeland.

The two men boarded the first goods train to leave Bordeaux. It seemed to be travelling east and the city of Strasbourg was chalked on some of the carriages, which was in the general direction of Celine's farm, a perfect alternative to the south west.

The exchange police transport had eventually arrived for the convicts two hours late and officers were shocked to see the dead bodies of two colleagues and the disappearance of the captives. The police quickly informed HQ and a road block was put in place stopping any transport travelling east or south. But they were too late. Jon was well on his way, his aim being to travel to the farm and seize it from Yvette. To save embarrassment the French police decided not to make the escape public but to engage specialist police to search, find and kill the two escapees.

WW1: THE NAKED SOLDIER

The train pulled into the railway sidings just outside Strasbourg just after dawn. The two fugitives cautiously left the train, climbed over a low wall and joined in with the flow of the early morning workers. It was easy in a big city to mingle in a crowd but with the pair having a limited amount of money they had choices to make. Jon decided to visit Yvette's farm and take possession of it by whatever means he could. Being a fugitive he reckoned that it would be unlikely for the police to link Jon with a farm on the other side of the country. The journey from Strasbourg to Nancy was 150 km which, if need be, they could walk in three days. The first day they walked north along the main road to Paris stopping off at villages along the way for food and drink. Just outside Saverne they were able to get a lift in the back of a truck travelling to Heillecourt, which was walking distance to Flavigny, the location of the farm.

They spent that night in a farmhouse inhabited by a couple who had lost their sons in the war. They showed great sympathy for two ex-soldiers who said that they were on the way to find work in the French reclaimed Alsace Lorraine area, having fought for two years against the Germans and helped reclaim the area back into French control. Jon told the couple a very convincing story and was rewarded with food, drink and a soft bed for the night.

The expected visit of the Basques came early the next day as Yvette and 'Jack' were working the butter churn. Fred, from his viewpoint, saw the two men coming and had his loaded rifle at the ready. It became obvious to Fred, after observing a heated discussion about ownership of the farm, that the men were readying themselves to kill 'Jack' and Yvette. As Jon raised his handgun in a threatening manner, Fred took careful aim and shot Jon in the chest. The other Basque man, not knowing the number or location of the defenders, took flight and ran in the direction of the outer barn. Having been taught to kill efficiently in the British Army and knowing that it would be dangerous for all of them if this man escaped, Fred found him and had no qualms in killing him. With both men now dead their bodies had to be disposed of.

Fred and 'Jack' still felt threatened as they assumed that there would be other visitors from Celine's adopted family. They decided that the best place to hide the bodies would be in the slurry tank at the rear of the farm. The drain from the tank had been sealed and had not been used since the two brothers had left the farm to fight in Verdun. With some difficulty the two men opened the lid and the three of them hauled the bodies inside the vessel. With the two men now disposed of the vessel was closed and the lid re-sealed.

Yvette and her two workers were now very aware that they would be receiving another visit from Celine's family and realised that their sustained vigilance would be critical over the following weeks and months. The stress of waiting for action became overwhelming, and after taking account of the options available to them, they decided than it was time to move on. An opportunity arose when the local farmer, seeing a positive future due to the increase in demand for the butter, cheese and the fresh produce that his farm had been well known for, asked to rent Yvette's farm.

A five-year rent with one year up front was agreed at a very reasonable price and the three took an option of going to find work with Sonia, a cousin of Yvette's, who lived with her husband, Albert, near Delle on the French/Swiss border. Here they could relax and consider the future.

Celine, having had no news of her husband and his friends, had resigned herself to the probability that they had all been killed in the ambush by the French police and the body of Jon, the leader, had been disposed of somewhere to avoid some grand burial ceremony and wake afterwards. Her intention was to return to the farm and claim what was rightfully hers but, finding herself pregnant, she actually settled down to the role of widowed young mother, which was not uncommon after the end of the war.

CHAPTER 14:
DELLE

A few eyebrows were raised at the sight of a young woman travelling alone with two young men and envious glances came from women in their the mid to late twenties who were living alone with young children, having lost their husbands during the war.

'How is this woman, this cousin of Sonia's, living with two men when we have none?' they muttered to themselves.

Even the explanation of one of the men being her husband and the other being her husband's cousin did not quell the feelings of jealousy.

Once the three became involved in village life, they found themselves made very welcome, particularly the two men who had fought for France's freedom.

To keep up appearances, 'Jack' and Yvette acted the part of man and wife. It was a role that both became very comfortable with and eventually the act became reality. Fred suspected that the two had become closer as he watched them working together on the farm and in the fields. Fred was not involved in the day to day discussions between the two, which were carried out in French. At first 'Jack' would translate for Fred, but as time went on this became more infrequent. The three contributed greatly to the overall running of Sonia's husband's farm and they all settled down to a happy lifestyle. The only drawback was the lack of communication with Sonia's husband, Albert, who kept himself aloof from Fred, 'Jack' and Yvette. It seemed that he only tolerated the trio to keep his wife happy. He was considerably older than Sonia and it was assumed, by virtue of the local gossip, that he had previously been married and that his wife had died in very tragic circumstances. Albert avoided discussing his past as it brought back memories that he didn't wish to talk about. He had met Sonia fifteen years ago at a mutual friend's wedding. Both were single and after a brief courtship they married. Albert bought the farm from a local agent and had employed experienced agriculture workers on the land while he worked for Peugeot. Initially the business sold bicycles and then later sold automobiles as the motor car became more popular and affordable to many business men who were only too keen to show off this modern means of transportation. He had built a close relationship with Armand Peugeot, with whom he had discussed the implementation of the social reforms that put Peugeot's working conditions way ahead of any other factory in France.

The war had changed the production emphasis at the Peugeot factory from private automobiles to assisting in the war effort by supplying a range of vehicles to satisfy the needs of the French and Allied armies. The war had benefitted Albert greatly and not always in conventional ways. Now that the conflict was over he was planning to expand his business into exclusively selling, servicing and repairing Peugeot automobiles having sold off the interest he had in bicycles. He saw the great potential in automobiles replacing horse-drawn vehicles as well as posing a challenge to the railway systems throughout the industrialised world.

Having five adults living together under the same roof resulted in minor conflict and irritation between them, but they all made efforts to overcome any difference in opinion. 'Jack' thought that there was something usual about Albert but he couldn't decide what it was. This was confirmed when he heard Albert quietly swearing under his breath: a crude German word addressed to one of the bookkeeping staff. Albert came back with an apology saying that the word was something that he'd heard a German POW say to one of the guards.

Albert purposely steered himself away from becoming too friendly with people in general as he found making conversation with anyone other than his close personal friends and his family very difficult. 'Jack' tried to enter into a discussion about the future of the motor car, but he received little encouragement. Albert's family was French from Colmar and Sonia was his second wife. The marriage to Sonia was childless but, if the gossipmongers in the local bars were to be believed, Albert had children with his first wife.

It was only supposition, however, because Albert never discussed his past. It had been suggested in one local bar that his parents were in fact German and Albert had some means of communicating with them. This had been guessed at and assumed by many in the village, particularly the locals in the station bar. It was well known that Albert went on an overnight business trip every two weeks. He told his wife that he could not disclose his business due to state security but a couple of the local men came up with a theory that he was visiting a lady friend or perhaps, wife, somewhere in the mountains and spending a night with her and probably, seeing his children. 'Yes, he is,' said one of the men who had worked on Albert's farm, 'and the lady in question is his German-born wife.'

There were many men who thought Albert's aloofness was evidence that he had something to hide, but everyone in the village loved Sonia so the village community decided to ignore the issues with her husband.

Yvette became concerned that even though she was in a relationship with 'Jack' she still had to be discreet about their relationship by having separate rooms. It would not take much guessing as to what happened most nights, though, confirmed by creaky floor boards and an old metal framed bed.

Yvette had spoken to Sonia about Fred's loneliness and asked Sonia if there was anyone in the village they could match with Fred. Sonia and Yvette went through the names of war widows in the village and surrounding area but could not put a name to anyone suitable mainly due to language difference. Sonia thought about the matter over the following week.

Else Berner was born in Boncourt, on the Swiss side of the border with France, and had lived there until she met and married a friend of Sonia's from the French village of Delle. Else's husband, Claude, had been called up in 1917 to help with the logistics of getting men and material from the factory and transferring goods and equipment to the various stocking areas. He had previously been a component buyer for Peugeot and hadn't expected to play an active part in the war. Unfortunately, he was involved in an accident, caught between two vehicles trying to pass each other at maximum speed.. Claude was thrown from his vehicle directly into the path of the oncoming vehicle and suffered major injuries. He was immediately transferred to a hospital but he eventually died. Else was devastated and through diplomatic arrangement in a time of war she was allowed to cross the border back to her homeland of Switzerland.

Sonia had recently received a letter from Else saying that she wanted to return to France and to her husband's village where she had such happy memories. Else had not sold or rented her house near Delle, so she could technically return to France now that the borders had been re-opened.

By the end of the month Else had returned to her husband's village and planned to stay with Sonia and Albert for just a short time. As Sonia only had four bedrooms she had to ask Yvette if she would share Jack's room, leaving a room free for her new guest. Yvette was only too pleased to co-operate with the new arrangement.

Fred was happy to hear about the new English speaking guest. Before Else's marriage to Claude, she had been an English teacher at a Young Ladies Finishing School in Biel/Bienne. This large industrial town was in the middle of the French/German-speaking parts of Switzerland, where it was said that one side of the street spoke French and the other side spoke German. A solution, discussed in the town, suggested to change the dual language to a single language: English.

It wasn't just Fred who was heartened by the news of Else's imminent arrival back in the village, it was especially good news to Artur, the owner and manager of the local grocery store which also acted as a Post Restante, receiving and sending letters on behalf of residents who, for whatever reason, did not want post delivered to their home address. Artur, in his responsibility as postmaster was aware of a letter arriving from Switzerland for Sonia and he guessed that it must be from Else.

Artur had been best man at the wedding of Claude and Else and remained unmarried as he was still waiting for the lady of his dreams to come along. In the meantime Artur's romantic activities were well known as he frequently visited a young married woman in the next village whose husband was held at a German prisoner of war camp in Bavaria. Artur had assumed that Else would return back to the marital home. He was disappointed to learn that she was to stay with her friend Sonia and her brusque and unfriendly husband who were now joined by two soldiers, who he knew nothing about, and her cousin from the Nancy region, called Yvette. Nothing happened in the village and surrounding areas without Artur knowing about it and what he was not sure of, he made a calculated guess at.

As time went on the four friends seemed to have a happy time together and Else enjoyed having someone to talk to. On their weekly visit into the village, Else would go into Artur's store on the pretence of buying bits and pieces. Artur would invite Else into his office and they would have coffee and cake while recalling stories about the good times the three friends had had together. Artur would relate to Else of the good times he and Claude had shared as boys, teenagers and young men, then he and Else would speak of how they both still missed Claude. Else would leave Artur after her brief visit and join her three friends at the local bar. This annoyed Artur.

'Why could she not spend a bit more time with him instead of sitting and laughing with the English soldier, if that is what he was,' Artur muttered to himself.

While the trio were enjoying a peaceful life in the mountains, however, events were starting to unfold which would have a direct effect on their lives.

CHAPTER 15:
PARIS NIGHTCLUB

The troops who had fought in the war were demobilised over a lengthy period and, once they had taken their pay, they tended to want to spend time in Paris before going back to what would be in many cases a mundane existence. The celebrations had started with the release of soldiers from duty soon after hostilities ceased. It had been decided by the wise generals and 'learned' politicians that the latest recruits should be demobilised first. This policy was based on the theory that there would be less disruption back in the workplaces as some of these lads had only left their employment three months before. This decision was typical of the disrespect and lack of recognition for those soldiers who had fought for up to four years and had not seen their families for many months and, in some cases, for the duration of the war.

A small group of returning British and Commonwealth soldiers were heard boasting, in a bar near the Eiffel Tower, about how they had avoided carnage on the western front while their French, American and British comrades were being killed and maimed. As they consumed more and more drink, their stories indicated that these men had hidden away from harm in a cellar rather than do their duty and engage with the enemy. The editor of the London Telegraph, who happened to be on a conference trip to Paris, overheard the story. The conference had been organised to discuss the newsworthiness of allegations that both sides in the conflict had committed atrocities including an alleged story that a British soldier had been nailed to a barn door and crucified.

This story had been told to the Telegraph by a returning soldier who had allegedly seen the dead man hanging from a door; he claimed to know of someone who had a picture of it but he wanted £100 for it. Although this apparent crucifixion was staged to make money, it was just one of the incredible stories, the merits of which were to be discussed by British, French and American newspaper people. They would then come to an agreement on a common strategy for investigating and verifying all such stories coming from the war.

At the conference several servicemen had been invited to give evidence regarding the credulity or otherwise of some fifty stories. The conference comprised of six national newspaper's editing staff with each having a clerical assistant present to take notes.

Three members of the BRU were invited to attend but could only be spared for one night due to the high volume of work they still had to deal with. The spokesman for the BRU at the conference was to be Joe Riley. Joe had been awarded a senior position in the unit as a reward for his work ethic and for the dedication he showed while working in very difficult conditions

Many stories from the conference related to parts of dead soldiers bodies being taken as mementoes, ears being considered by some units of the German army as direct evidence of a kill. Members of the BRU re-iterated the 'ear' stories but when Joe Riley stood up to tell of his experience, the members were astonished to hear his story of the naked soldier whose identity could not be established. Questions were fired at Joe regarding the circumstances surrounding this story and how much time had been dedicated to investigating such an unusual case. Joe explained the procedure that had to be followed for this and any other retrieval.

'According to my personal notes, written alongside the official report, the face of the soldier had suffered severe injury and no positive identification would have been possible and as the body was completely naked, there were no personal effects to help me with identification. There was not a lot of time available, due to the amount of work we had to do with body retrieval, trying to identify fallen soldiers, taking notes of their units and numbers then transporting them to dedicated burial plots. We did not have much time to allocate to any single individual. However, in the little spare time I had I was intrigued by the circumstances relating to the naked soldier. I visited Perone and got a five minute interview with the cathedral chaplain. He confirmed that he knew the story of the naked body as he had personally attended the burial and he showed me the grave where the body was interred. The identification process allows a maximum of five items of information. The name of the soldier, his regiment, his serial number, the date he fell and the area the action took place. In relation to this soldier we had no name, serial number or regiment but we could establish the area where he was fighting and the date he fell which was the 29 September 1918. A simple stone had been placed at the head of his resting place in the Churchyard in Perone and had the words 'Here lies a brave solider known only to God'.

The meeting discussed various allegations but the two that took up the most time were the case of the naked soldier and the boasting by returning soldiers about hiding from battle. This act, if proven, would mean a court martial for anyone that could be identified from that particular bar. This possible outcome of court martial was documented so no further discussion was needed.

In conclusion, the editors considered the potential desertion story to be the more interesting and newsworthy so that was the one chosen for publication. The editors agreed, however, only to publish after all the facts were gathered and once that was complete, the story would be published the same day by each newspaper with no one jumping the gun.

The chairman of the committee thanked Joe Riley for the information he had given and offered thanks on behalf of all those at the meeting for the difficult and emotionally challenging work that the BRU carry out. The whole meeting proceeded to then stand up in a show of appreciation for the BRU and all their members. The meeting closed and arrangements commenced.

At the date set by the editors, all the newspapers printed the story of how boastful British soldiers had laughed and joked about hiding away during a forward thrust against German defences, while their fellow troops were getting mowed down by machine gun fire. The newspaper included details of how the soldiers, who had survived that initial machine gun onslaught, had to then go on and engage in hand-to-hand fighting with the enemy.

The article was printed on the front pages with the headlines: 'Who are these men, these cowards?'

Details were given of the name of the bar in Paris and one English newspaper asked the question 'What should be done to identify these men and shouldn't the army allocate resources to trace them?' Apart from a boastful act of cowardice, those involved brought shame on all officers and men of the British and Commonwealth armed forces. After the article had appeared so prominently in the major journals, the local and provincial newspapers took up the challenge with the same question 'Who are these cowards?'

There were rumours that, in the last weeks of the war, young soldiers decided that to risk being killed or maimed, when everyone knew the end of the war was imminent, was a fool's game. These soldiers had more than done their duty: they were not cowards and had fought bravely during the advancement at the end of September and the beginning of October.

Some senior officers had considered it futile for generals to send young men to their death when some face-to-face negotiations could end the conflict.

Would the generals get stuck in and pick up a rifle? No chance of that. They were too comfortable spending the war in some confiscated chateau a safe distance from the action.

The Parisian article, printed in UK newspapers, brought home the tragedy of all the husbands, brothers and sons who had been killed during the four years of conflict. As people read the article, the 'letters to the editor' section gathered momentum. There were many letters sent to the newspapers.

A lady from Birmingham, who had lost two sons in the Somme offensive in 1917 and a brother in the first week of November 1918, wrote to her MP demanding that an investigation be carried out to establish whether there was any truth in the possibility that there were deserters living in France and that, if there were, these cowards needed to be brought to justice without delay.

A mother from Kirby who had received a letter from her son dated 10 November had not heard anything since. She didn't know if he was alive, living in France, having deserted or if he had been killed on the last day. 'Do those lads in Paris know Reg from Liverpool?'

A lady from Norfolk wrote in about her fiancé, who had been killed two weeks before their wedding and was heartbroken at losing her one love whom she had known since infant school and now was no longer alive.

Another young woman's letter told of how she had just had her first baby when news came about her twin brother being captured by the Germans and had received no news since. 'What has happened to the other half of me? Why has he not returned? Is there anything I can do to find him?'

Such was the despair and heartache suffered as a result of the newspaper article.

CHAPTER 16:
ARTUR

The headlines in the major newspapers in France eventually filtered down to the provincial newspapers and then down to the local journals. Artur, who was intensely jealous of the British soldiers and their closeness to Else, started to discuss the details of the newspaper article with those who came into his shop. 'Isn't it disgusting what has happened in Paris! Those British soldiers bragging about hiding while the French fought the Germans.' He made no reference to Sonia's visitors in his discussions: he let village gossip take root and watched the subject become the main talking point in the local bar.

It took little time for one of the locals to ask questions about Sonia's guests. One of the farmers started the debate.

'Does anyone have any idea what they did in the war and why they are still here in France?'

Another remarked that Sonia had told his wife that they had carried out some heroic deeds in the Argonne and had been honoured with some prestigious American medal but had turned it down because they said that their success was a team effort, it was not down to any individuals.

'Well, I can't make my mind up whether they are brave soldiers or just plain stupid,' a retired soldier said while drinking in a local bar. 'According to a story I heard, the American Army had apparently offered them a lot of money through some rich gentleman whose only son had been saved by these two soldiers during a raid on a prison block where hundreds of Americans had been encircled.'

'Be that the case,' replied a father who had lost his son while fighting in Verdun, 'it's still very strange. What do you think, Artur?'

Artur had just closed his shop and walked into the bar. 'What do I think of what?' Artur replied. 'I'm not sure what you were talking about.'

The man said, 'I'm talking about the two soldiers who live with your girlfriend, or who you would like to be your girlfriend. Seems like you have had your nose pushed out.'

The bar filled with laughter at that suggestion and Artur, who was embarrassed, quickly downed his wine then excused himself, saying he had work to do.

'That touched a raw nerve,' one of the farmers quipped as he finished the dregs of his coffee and Armagnac.

Artur decided that the next time he visited the main local town he would have a word with the desk sergeant, who he knew well, to see if the police knew anything about these two men staying with Sonia and Albert. Like most subjects discussed in the bar, however, the desertion story ran its course and after two days it was forgotten.

It was a further two weeks before Artur had need to go into town and, after finishing some business, he went into the local gendarmerie and asked to see the sergeant. The constable on the desk, who knew Artur, asked him to sit down and wait until the sergeant was free.

Artur was eventually welcomed by the sergeant and asked if he would like a small cognac. Once the drinks were poured the sergeant asked, 'What is troubling you, Artur?'

Artur explained about the article in the newspaper relating to the drunken outburst from some English soldiers in Paris saying that they hidden while French soldiers were getting killed and maimed.

The sergeant nodded. 'Yes, I read the article and I have been informed by the department that an investigation will be carried out throughout France to establish the facts and the extent of the problem; that is if there is a problem.' The sergeant looked closely at his companion. 'Is there something specific that concerns you, Artur?'

'Well, yes there is,' replied Artur, at which the sergeant asked for specific details of his concerns.

Artur told the story of the two soldiers, one English and one from the British Commonwealth, who were staying with Sonia, the wife of Albert the Automobile enthusiast.

'Can I stop you there please, Artur?' the sergeant interrupted. 'These two soldiers you are talking about. One of them from England and one from New Zealand? Both of them came to my office less than a week ago and explained that they had seen the article in the local newspaper. It had suggested to them, by one of the occasional helpers on the farm where they are working, that they should go to the gendarmerie in town office and give details relating to their extended stay. Both men came with a letter from General Johnson of the United States Army explaining the details of their action and the very positive results they achieved, having rescued imprisoned soldiers who had been treated badly by their German captors and were in extremely poor physical condition. The letter went on to say that they were being considered for a special bravery medal from the United States; that one of those rescued by these two soldiers was a rich man's only son and that a substantial monetary reward has been offered to the two soldiers in return for their efforts.'

Artur was impressed with the citation but added, 'One thing that I find strange, though, is that occasionally one of the men, Fred, calls the other one Fritz when his name is Jack. Why in a war against Germany would you want to give someone a German name? Even if it is a nickname.'

The sergeant replied, ' It was probably a joke nickname, possibly relating to his ancestors having come from Germany many years ago. There are many Americans with German ancestors and still have German surnames, although most have now Americanised them.'

At that Artur finished his cognac and bid farewell. After Artur left, the sergeant discussed the details of the meeting with his constable and said that, actually, he was intrigued as to why you would call someone Fritz when his name was Jack. 'Strange, isn't it?'

Artur's jealousy continued and matters came to a head after Else had been to her bank in town and stood behind the police sergeant in a queue of people waiting to be served.

'Your friend Artur seems a bit upset with your friend Sonia's British lodgers,' the sergeant commented.

Else was taken aback and replied, 'I don't understand, I was with Artur yesterday having a coffee and he never mentioned anything about Fred, if that is who he is concerned about. Fred is a really nice man and I have no idea what could possibly concern Artur.'

'Perhaps he is jealous,' replied the sergeant. 'Maybe he thought that you and Artur might get together some time and feels the British man has supplanted him in your affections.'

'Sorry,' said Else, 'there has never been anything between me and Fred other than mutual friendship. If I was thinking of getting involved with another man, which I am not, then Fred would be the type of man I would consider. Not some shopkeeper who runs to the police and makes up stories to suit his own purpose.'

At that Else bid the sergeant good day and returned home.

Fred realised that Else was upset when she did not come down that evening to eat the dinner Sonia had prepared. It had left just four at the table as Albert had gone on one of his periodic 'business' trips.

Else did come down but much later, just as the group were clearing the table and getting ready to retire for the night. Sonia,

Yvette and 'Jack' went to their rooms, leaving Fred stirring the last of the embers in the fireplace, but just as he was ready to retire to his room Else approached him.

'Fred,' Else said, 'I had a strange experience when I was in town today.' She continued to explain the events of the day, her discussion with the police sergeant and the facts relating to the sergeant's meeting with Artur, the shop keeper.

Else asked Fred for his opinion on what Artur had said and the implication that she and Fred had some sort of relationship. 'It's not three years since I lost Claude and the pain is still with me each and every day. But I am still young and I will at some stage find friendship again and if I did I would like someone like you, Fred, but not at the moment. I'm sure that you can understand my feelings.'

'Of course.' Fred nodded. 'I fully understand, I have no wife or lady friend waiting for me back home and I am happy working on the farm and living with Sonia and Albert, seeing and talking to you each day. Sometime in the future we can talk about getting to know each other better. But for now, I'm happy, if you wish, to just leave things as they are.'

The next day Else went to visit Artur and told him that she had seen the police sergeant and had discussed the two soldiers in regard to the newspaper article about desertion and how Artur had tried to imply it related to Fred and Jack.

'I'm bitterly disappointed in you, Artur. You've got a lot of nerve to say you are my friend. I did not think that you were a malicious type of person, but now I see you as you really are and you're no good. Thank you for your coffee and cake but please do not expect me to visit you again. You have let both Claude and I down: my husband only ever saw you as a true friend but to do what you have done is not the action of a true friend. Good day to you.'

CHAPTER 17:
MICHEL ETXARRI

In the southwest corner of France, bordering Spain, the end of the war had the effect of calming the relationship between the local police and the Basque population. Celine was still unsure of what had become of her husband. Her days were taken up caring for her son, Jon. There had been no news about her husband and so she concluded that he had initially escaped but was later captured by the French police. Under orders from HQ in Paris, an easy option would be to kill Jon then dispose of his body in order to save any publicity about an escape from custody.

Celine contacted a Spanish policeman, Sergeant Michel Etxarri, and asked for help in finding out what had happened to her husband. Michel attended monthly meetings with Basque elders in San Sebastian as a liaison officer in order to discuss any cross border issues that might have arisen. Celine's husband, Jon, had been trusted to ensure that his friends and associates maintained the respect of the mutual authority of the French, Spanish and Basque communities. In return, Jon was given some latitude in carrying out some traditional cross border activities such as poaching for wild boars: the meat and offal of these animals being considered a delicacy by the mountain people, but unfortunately these wild 'pigs' had no respect for the borders of the three communities and often had to be pursued deep into foreign territory.

Michel's parentage was Basque on his mother's side and French on his father's. His father worked for an international bank in Spanish speaking Burgos and due to Michel spending the school summer holidays with his grandparents, he became tri-lingual speaking French, Spanish and Euskadi. He joined the Spanish police after studying history at Leon University and was soon recognised as an asset who could help with the occasional difficult issues that arose during the meetings between the three communities.

Celine arranged a meeting with Michel at the police HQ in Irun. It was suggested by the elders that she should be accompanied by one of Jon's close friends and so the eldest son of a local farmer, who was unknown to the police, went with her as the meeting was potentially tricky and Celine did not trust that the police wouldn't ask questions unrelated to the request for information about Jon.

Celine had just two questions for the policeman:

'If he was killed in the conflict in the mountains then where is his body?' and,

'If he has been arrested, may I know where he is?'

She looked earnestly at Michel. 'I am very distressed, as I do not know whether I have a husband or not and my child does not know if he has a daddy. Please will you help us? What can I do to find out what has happened to my Jon?'

The Spanish policeman was sympathetic towards Celine's plight, having, the year before lost his wife to the Asian Flu.

Michel explained to Celine that he could not be seen to be helping the wife of a murderer. He told Celine that he would look into the matter and suggested that they could meet in a hotel in San Sebastian. Celine realised that the officer had an ulterior motive in getting her to this hotel but considered that it was probably the only way she would find the truth about her husband.

The meeting was arranged at the Hotel Londres and while they were together Michel arranged for her chaperone to be escorted to a bar in the old town and be distracted with drink and tapas.

During the ensuing afternoon of passion, Celine found out that Jon had escaped from the French police but no further trace of him had been found and learnt that he was still wanted by the French police for murder.

After the interlude at the hotel, the police officer suggested that he would discreetly find out as much as he could before their next meeting, which was arranged to be the last day of the following month. In the meantime, if either of them had any news about Jon they were to keep in contact. They agreed that he would keep their friendship a secret from his family in Spain and she would keep it a secret from her people in the mountains.

Celine realised that if Jon had escaped, he would have most likely made his way to the family farm. Celine decided that, as she had unfinished business with Yvette, she would find an excuse to leave her home, put her son in the care of Jon's family then ask one of Jon's friends go with her for support.

CHAPTER 18:
REMEMBRANCE

The anniversary of the end of the fighting came to pass and thoughts of those who had been killed fighting for king and country were uppermost in people's thoughts. Those who had laid down their lives. Perhaps a son, a husband, a brother, a fiancé, a cousin or close friend. The actions of these brave men were foremost in the minds of the bereaved. A debate ensued as to how the public should recognise the sacrifice of the fallen. Each city, town and village wanted a memorial to commemorate the duty and commitment of those who had lost their lives fighting for 'our freedom'. Many of the centres of population decided to form a committee of prominent people such as local merchants, but more importantly the soldiers who had been there to witness the carnage.

Some of the larger towns and cities were opting for an elaborate memorial: considered as a fitting tribute to the fallen. Some of the smaller towns and villages were considering a simple memorial: a single column with the names of the fallen inscribed on a plaque. There was a suggestion of planting flowers and providing a seat or a tasteful garden bench where people could sit and remember. The possibilities were limitless.

In Canterbury, New Zealand, a panel of twelve people had been selected, comprising of four soldiers, a mother, a wife, four prominent businessmen, the lord mayor and the chief of police: a fine group of responsible people together with those who had the deepest pockets and would have the most say as to what should be decided.

Through the local news media, posters, clubs, societies and through the church committees of various denominations, a selection of ten memorial proposals was made. The twelve panellists were asked to comment on all ten. The selection procedure was intense and the vote came out as being equal for two of the options.

The first was of a mother sheltering her two young children from an oncoming German soldier. This option contained very detailed facial expressions: the German soldier's features were snarled as he went in for the kill while the mother's face was defiant as she covered both children with her cloak and grasped a large knife in a hand hidden from the soldier's view. This option was dramatic and there were discussions about variations of this theme up and down Britain and throughout the Empire.

The second option was based on a true action that had happened during the advance on the Hindenburg Line at the end of September 1918. The story had been the subject of an article in the local Evening Post. In fairly graphic detail, it showed two soldiers right in front of a machine gun post each with a grenade in his hand, with two soldiers each side backing up the central attack.

It was a difficult choice because both were very emotional pieces of work. One was fictional; one was real.

The selection process was lengthy. The best sculptor had to be chosen, the best possible design artist had to be considered and the best accountant had to be found in order to collate and manage the collected funds.

The city hall was to be the venue for the final meeting of the Christchurch Memorial Committee. The 'raid on machine gun post' was the preferred option of the editor and director of the local newspaper as it was for two of the soldiers who had been part of the action. 'The mother protecting her children' was proposed by the Women's Guild of the New Zealand Anglican Church.

A decision process was agreed upon with each of the twelve members being asked to choose between either: A: the 'Mother' or B: the 'Raid'.

The two soldiers informed the rest of the committee that they should abstain as they had been directly involved in the raid on the machine gun post.

The voting process started with the remaining two soldiers.

Soldier 1 voted for B
Soldier 2 voted for B
The mother voted for A
The wife voted for A
Businessman 1 voted for A
Businessman 2 voted for A
Businessman 3 voted for B
Businessman 4 voted for B
The chief of police abstained

This left four votes for A and four votes for B with the lord mayor being left with the casting vote.

Now having this responsibility thrown directly onto him and him alone, he asked the committee if he could have a brief meeting with the two soldiers who abstained, together with the wife and the mother. This was granted and the five went to a side room where the mayor asked each one of them to tell him which of the two proposals might be most meaningful to those visiting the site on the 11 November 2018, in one hundred years' time. This question was debated by all four of them and they soon agreed that B would be the one to tell the story to their great, great grandchildren. The meeting closed and all concerned walked the one hundred yards together to the Rose of Lancaster public house and proposed a drink to the brave men who fought at the machine gun post at the end of September 1918.

After the Armistice had been celebrated, life started to get back to normal: troops had been allowed to go back home and the maimed and badly injured were being treated and rehabilitated. The names of the dead were recorded and wherever possible a name was given to identify with a body. It became an unpalatable fact that even with the tremendous efforts of the BRU, only a minority of the fallen actually had the correct name with the correct body. But that was due to the conditions of war, the results of the battle, the state of the battlefield, the time lag in body retrieval and the constant barrage of shells churning up shell-holed ground.

The US Awards Committee was established soon after the cessation of activities in November 1918. The committee had been tasked to sift through hundreds of citations from US officers giving details of extreme deeds of bravery: bravery over and above what could be expected from even the most experienced soldiers. It became a mammoth task to consistently assess each of the citations and to apply a standard for evaluation. The initial assessors had been schoolmasters, policemen and semi-retired businessmen. The war citation committee had put pressure on these assessors to present an initial report on each of the files that they had been working on. To help speed the process, a ten point evaluation was to be used with a half point split to help with cases that seemed identical.

After the initial six months' work, the assessment teams had produced a consolidated schedule of soldiers who came out classified at a level of 8.0 plus. This schedule alone contained one hundred and twenty-six names.

To satisfy the timescale of planned visit to Paris by Mr Woodrow Wilson, the president of the United States, a summary document was drafted that would give him enough time to read out the name, rank and unit of each of the citations classified as 9.0 and above. He would then add a brief ten to fifteen word statement explaining the action each soldier had been involved in and, finally, the name of a top senior official who had sanctioned the citation.

Herbert Smith, the editor of the daily and evening editions of the Canterbury Post in New Zealand, was on an extended visit to Great Britain, France and Turkey to see for himself how the carnage of the recent conflict had devastated soldiers and civilians.

The editor, while not personally writing articles in his newspapers, was ultimately responsible for all printed matter, the quality of presentation, the accuracy of content and the maintenance of overall standards: standards that had been nurtured over the sixty years the newspaper had been in print.

Herbert took a great interest in events relating to the recent world war having lost his own nephew to a sniper's bullet on the 10 November.

The New Zealand Memorial Committee assessed the options and finalised their selections. Herbert was pleased with the final two selected and he was particularly happy with the choice of the 'Raid' as he had written part of the article about that event himself and had been very engaged with most of the research. He had sat in on an interview with two of the soldiers involved in the attack of the machine gun post and was impressed by the way each man had put credit for the mission's success fairly and squarely on the shoulders of a Sergeant Jack Jackson and a Lance Corporal George Mills.

Two of the other soldiers involved in the raid had returned to their homes in a remote part of the North Island and did not want to talk about the war as both still had nightmares about the man-to-man fighting they had had to engage in. Herbert was aware that Sergeant Jackson had been killed during the course of the battle and that George Mills had probably returned to his family in England. He had decided that during his visit to England he would try to arrange a meeting with George Mills. He knew that his regiment was the Duke of Cornwall's Light Infantry, so contact with the DCLI HQ in Bodmin, Cornwall would be a starting point.

By coincidence, the visit to Paris of the president of the United States coincided with Mr and Mrs Herbert's own visit to the French capital. Through contacts at the British and Commonwealth embassy, Herbert and his wife were invited to the American award ceremony in order to represent the people of New Zealand and to reflect on the disproportionate loss of life the NZEF troops had suffered during the four years of fighting.

A schedule of events had been prepared. There was a list of one hundred and twenty-six soldiers who had been mentioned in citations but the list given to the president contained just twenty names.

After a light lunch for two hundred guests, the president spoke of the gratitude the American people had for all of those who had fought for freedom. He went on to say that he had selected twenty soldiers whose actions had represented the bravery of the US soldiers and their attachments. One by one the president, in a clear and distinguished voice, detailed the deeds of each of the twenty in alphabetical order.

A shiver went down the spine of Herbert Smith when Jack Jackson of the NZEF, attached to the US 77th Division, was mentioned with an account of his heroic actions carried out with the help of an unmentioned British colleague to rescue imprisoned US soldiers.

Herbert knew that Jack Jackson had been the name of the sergeant who had led the raid on the `machine gun post' and that he had lost his life carrying out that successful attack. The same man couldn't possibly have been killed in one action on the 29 September and then been part of a successful rescue mission some seven days later. The name and the unit were the same for both events. But, how could one man be in two places? Something unusual must have happened. A mix up with names perhaps. That was a distinct possibility considering the scale of the Allied actions around that period. The action at the end of September 1918 into October had come to be known as the 'The Final Push' to defeat Germany and end the war.

Herbert made a promise to himself that he would find out what had happened to Sergeant Jack Jackson. Intrigued by what he had seen and heard at the dinner, Herbert was eager to get back to his hotel and think about the possibilities surrounding this brave soldier and so left the event early. Herbert and his wife thanked the organisers and left on the pretence that his wife was coming down with the flu, resulting in Herbert missing the ongoing informal speeches.

Of particular interest was a speech delivered by Mr Joseph Van de Veldt, a billionaire, industrial magnate from Newport, Rhode Island, who spoke of his gratitude to the two soldiers who had rescued captured US troops trapped in the Argonne Forest. He told guests, 'I am a man of great wealth but it would be worth nothing without my only son to carry on my work. I would like to offer a financial reward or I should say, compensation, to these two soldiers but I, even with my resources, am not able trace them. So, if any of you find out that they have heard of my search, please tell Jack Jackson and George Mills to contact me through any newspaper and I will get back to them.'

On returning to the hotel, Herbert explained to his wife about the remarkable coincidence regarding Jack Jackson. 'Two Jack Jacksons would be possible, but two Jack Jacksons in the same regiment fighting in the same area of conflict, although not impossible, is highly unlikely.' Herbert determined that he would strengthen his efforts to find Lance Corporal George Mills when he visited England the following week.

CHAPTER 19:
GEORGE MILLS

The city of Canterbury commissioned Brendan Peters, a sculptor, to design and construct the memorial to the fallen, and two soldiers who had been part of the 'Raid' were invited to participate in the modelling of the memorial. The artist had to be creative to ensure all the details of the six soldiers stood out. They had to be shown as a cluster, although in reality the soldiers were some distance apart. One of the soldiers suggested that the body of Sergeant Jack Jackson should be exhumed, transported from France then be interred under the monument as a token of the commitment that himself and thousands of others had shown on the various battlefields.

The committee wrote to the War Graves Commission to ask that the body of Jack Jackson be re-interred as part of a memorial to the fallen who had served and fought for the British Empire. After making several requests to the French War Graves Commission to locate the body of the fallen soldier, the reply came back that they had no record of a Jack Jackson. If the location of the action was in the British sector then they suggested that they contact the British War Graves Commission.

The committee sent a letter to the HQ of the War Graves Commission asking if they had any record of a Jack Jackson of the NZEF who was killed in action on the 29 or 30 of September 1918. The letter was received and acknowledged but then filed with all the other hundreds of similar letters asking for someone to be traced. Details of requests relating to fallen New Zealand soldiers were printed in the personal page of the Canterbury Post.

Herbert Smith, in England, did not see the name of Jack Jackson printed in his paper. He had, however, been able to trace the whereabouts of Lance Corporal George Mills. Herbert made a request to see George but, as George was working that day, an arrangement had had to be made through the Management of the Asia Mill on Clayton Street in Hollinwood, Manchester to allow an interview to take place. After his commitment and dedication to the war effort George had returned home to find employment as a Bobbin Carrier.

George's job was to move the reels of cotton slivers, produced on the carding machines on the first floor, up to the ring rooms on the second and third floors. In these departments the cotton would be spun on to tubes in the required 'counts' prior to being sold to weavers who would then produce the various qualities of cloth that would be made into garments and household goods. The work was simple and as such relatively low paid.

Due to company protocol, George had to be accompanied by the card room manager, Billy Lamb. Herbert was offered a cup of tea and though used to a china cup, Herbert did his best with the offered brew delivered in a chipped, pint-sized cup

He asked George questions about the 'Raid': how it was planned and how it was carried out. George gave Herbert graphic details of the fatal injury that Jack had suffered and how, with such little time available, they had only managed to partially bury the body. Coming under fire again they had had to leave Jack's body and move on to the next encounter. George was asked if he could recollect the location of the 'Raid' because that would help the WGC trace through their records and establish, if they could, what had happened to the body of Jack Jackson. Even if his face was destroyed he would still have had his dog tags with his name, rank and serial number.

George recalled the journey that day, setting off from the base just outside Villers-Plouich and finally reaching the Hindenburg Line behind the village of La Vacquerie with a goal of reaching and crossing the St Quentin Canal that formed part of the German defence line and how because of German resistance they had found themselves being driven south towards St Quentin. Herbert was very impressed with the way George conducted himself and asked for his address so he could communicate further if necessary. As the meeting concluded Herbert thanked George and Billy, apologising to Billy for letting the tea go cold.

While he was in England, Herbert thought it might prove fruitful to contact the HQ of the War Graves Commission (WGC) to see if they could offer any help as to the resting place of Jack Jackson. The Christchurch Memorial Committee efforts to locate Sergeant Jackson's body had been unsuccessful, despite having sought information from French government sources to establish what records would enable them to trace the location of the sergeant's body. So the next option was the WGC. Having key information from George Mills as to the approximate location of the 'Raid' it then became a painstaking exercise to sift through the reports submitted each day by the BRU. Concentrating on events around the 29 and 30 September they could not find the name of Jack Jackson. The records were searched again, this time by Herbert and the WGC officer looking to see if they could find the name Jack Jackson, but nothing was found. Herbert's eye clocked a record, which stated 'naked body'. 'What's the story relating to that?' Herbert asked. The officer took the notes from the file and read the details before checking to see what had happened to the body.

Could that body be Jack Jackson? If so, why was he naked and where was this body interred?

CHAPTER 20:

WER BIST DU / WHO ARE YOU?

Artur had not been put off by Else's rejection and had, in fact, become more vocal convincing the locals that the two men were probably deserters and that the citations were probably forged. One market day Sonia, 'Jack' and Yvette went on their own into the village.

While Sonia was visiting her doctor, 'Jack' and Yvette strolled through the village centre. They were shocked when an elderly man accused 'Jack' and Fred of being traitors and of being as bad as those in Paris. He followed this by spitting on the floor. They then went to the bar where they usually enjoyed a drink on the weekly market day but the barman refused to serve them.

Yvette was upset by the way they had been treated. 'Jack' shook his head and said quietly, 'It looks like it's time to move on.'

The local newspaper had detailed the outcome from the meeting of the Allied countries and the German Weimar Republic post-war government. The outcome was named 'The Treaty of Versailles' and it punished Germany both financially and strategically with France being given back lands lost in 1870, together with a 'buffer zone' giving the French land on the eastern, German side of the Rhine. The Alsace Lorraine area had been part of Germany for forty years until 1918. This meant that Jack's family were now part of France: good news for his mother but devastating for his father.

'Jack' looked at his options but knew he would take Yvette with him whatever he decided. He saw no benefit in continuing to stay with Sonia and Albert with potential trouble coming from Celine's Basque family who would almost certainly be back to claim the farm at some time in the future. He did, however, see opportunity in the new French lands of Alsace Lorraine. His French was now perfect and he could perhaps find a role for himself in the commercial sector. While still contemplating the future, Sonia's husband, Albert, walked through the door.

As he bid goodnight, 'Jack' asked Albert to stay with him for a while and have a drink in front of the fire. For the next hour 'Jack' asked Albert questions about the future of the motor car, questions Albert was happy to answer and told Jack that the automobile was the future while the days of the horse and cart were numbered. As the house went quiet Albert rose from the chair to bid 'Jack' goodnight but 'Jack' gestured for Albert to sit with him for a while longer and take a seat in front of the dying embers of the fire. Fritz looked Albert direct in his eyes and quietly said.

'ich Weiss war du bits und was du tuts, amber Albert, dean Geheimnis, ist bei mir sicher.'

Albert looked shocked. 'Jack' knew all about him but had said he would keep his secrets to himself. 'Jack' put his finger to his lips, said goodnight then climbed the stairs to bed.

'Jack' arranged to meet Albert to discuss one of his automobiles and to anyone looking on, it was just 'Jack' trying out one of Albert's cars. While driving he asked Albert if he could help discover the whereabouts of his parents and his two sisters who were living in what used to be Germany but now belonged to France. Albert tried explaining the difficulties of such a request but was galvanised into action by 'Jack' giving Albert just two weeks.

'Wer bist du?' Who are you? Albert asked; to which Jack replied, 'Nieman.' Nobody.

'Jack' explained to Albert that there were issues between Yvette and her sister-in-law over the ownership of her late husband's family farm. Her husband had been killed in Verdun and as he would not be returning, Yvette had registered the farm in her name. Since then it had been rented to a local farmer for a period of five years. Yvette's sister-in-law, Celine, had married into a Basque family who live in the mountains above Bayonne in south west France. These people were tribal and had vowed to get back what was Celine's birth right. The farmer renting Yvette's family farm knew that they were staying with Yvette's cousin. They were all aware that the Basque family's resources were such that they would search for him and Yvette, that they would be found and almost certainly killed. Yvette was concerned of the risks to herself, to Sonia and Albert, which is why they had made the decision to leave.

'Jack' explained that he would tell Fred of his and Yvette's decision but that they would not leave until Albert had discovered the whereabouts of his family.

'Jack' knew that the two weeks he had given was not long, but time was of the essence.

'My parents and sisters will be expelled from Alsace as part of the programme for the French to re-take what they have always considered to be part of their country.'

Albert listened intently. 'Jack' told Albert that he had no interest in his activities or why he appeared to be a 'German' living in France with a French wife. 'That is your business, but I repeat, you have two weeks to find where my parents and sisters are.'

On arriving back in the village, the two spent quite a while looking at the automobile and discussing its merits so as to not arouse any suspicion in those who might want to take an interest in what they were saying.

After a meal cooked by Sonia, 'Jack' said he had some news. He explained that Yvette and himself had decided to go to the Alsace Lorraine area where there were opportunities to find good paid work or to even set up a small business. He explained that they intended to leave in two weeks' time and asked Albert if he would drive them to Strasbourg where their quest for a new life would begin. For the first time, Albert spoke up at an evening meal. 'I realise that I am a quiet, private person and have not joined in the spirit of mutual enjoyment that the four of you and my lovely wife, Sonia, have engaged in. Jack and Yvette, I will take you as far as you wish and I will miss having you to stay. I regret that I was not as welcoming as I should have been. I wish you luck and good fortune in all your ventures.'

As each couple started to retire to their rooms Fred asked Else to stay a while. 'Else, I had no warning about what we have been told tonight and I'm as surprised as you. Jack and I have been together for three years and we have worked well both as friends and brothers. I now know what I would like to do and that is to ask you to marry me, but there is no rush for you to answer: I have some matters to sort out myself. Let's be patient with each other but let's plan for the future. So I'll say goodnight, my sweetheart, and I'll see you in the morning.'

Else went up to her room while Fred poked the ashes of the fire. After twenty minutes he went up but, on opening the door, the candle flickered on Else, who was standing at the side of his bed in her half opened nightdress. 'I am ready to spend the rest of my life with you,' she murmured. 'Whatever aspects of your life you need to sort out, I will be at your side, now and always, because without you I'm nothing. But let's not dwell on that at the moment. Let us concentrate on getting to know each other. We can talk in the morning.'

The following day, Fred told Else his story and described the circumstances in which he and 'Jack' had met. He explained that he and 'Jack', whose real name was Fritz, although on opposing sides, had both been born and brought up in the Manchester area. Rather than kill each other they took the decision to join forces, based on their belief that the war would be over within two days.

He explained how he had met 'Jack' and how he needed to get 'Jack', Fritz, out of his German uniform. They had selected a suitable dead Allied soldier, a NZ soldier, they unclothed him, and Fritz took the man's identity: that of Sergeant Jack Jackson. A decision was made to head for the Alsace region, an area Fritz, now 'Jack', was familiar with. On the road they met up with a party of recruits heading for the Meuse Argonne region. They followed the recruits and became involved in a mission to rescue 500 surrounded American troops, a mission which they carried out with great success. After the Armistice, they had continued on their journey, stopping off in a small town, south of Nancy where they got involved in an argument between Yvette and her sister-in-law, Celine. 'That resulted in us working on Yvette's farm and spending time bringing her farm back into operation. We became embroiled in a confrontation with Celine's new family from the Basque area and, knowing that her people would be back, we took the decision to move on and stay with Sonia. Which is where we are now. The problem we face is that the Basque people will find us and will harm us. The other issue we have is that Artur is turning the people in the village against us.'

Else considered everything, asking for clarification on some of the finer details of Fred's story. Fred told Else that 'Jack' carried on him the personal effects of the naked soldier and that he, Fred, had made a promise to return these to the dead soldier's family. This promise he would need to fulfil at some time in the future. Else suggested to Fred that he should ask 'Jack' for all the personal papers and letters belonging to 'Jack' Jackson because if 'Jack' was moving to the new zone he could have any identity he wished and would no longer need to be 'Jack Jackson'. The documents might prove useful to Fred in the future. She could take the papers with her when she visited her family village in Switzerland where she had to tidy up some business relating to Claude. While there, she could deposit the papers in her family's safe at the local bank.

Fred was happy with this and Else suggested that she could ask the sergeant in the town for his advice on what they should do. She told Fred that she knew the sergeant very well and could trust both his integrity and confidentiality.

CHAPTER 21:
LEAVING DELLE

At the end of the two-week period that 'Jack' had given Albert to discover the whereabouts of his family he decided that it was time to move from Delle to 'pastures new'. Yvette packed a minimum of clothes and some personal items for their departure the next morning. Albert had informed 'Jack' that he had news relating to his family and would give them the details the next day when they were in the car. Goodbyes were said and promises to meet up soon were given and as a final gesture 'Jack' handed Fred a sealed envelope. 'This contains the personal papers of Jack Jackson. I have written a statement detailing how we met on the battlefield and the time we have spent together since.'

Fred thanked Fritz and gave the envelope to Else for safekeeping.

Albert had the car ready for an early start and after a light breakfast the trio began their journey.

As Albert started his conversation about Jack's family he only just avoided hitting the local postman, almost knocking him off his bike. The postman waved for Albert to stop but Albert just gave a courteous wave back. The postman had with him an urgent message for Yvette telling her that the farmer, to whom she had rented her farm, had received visitors claiming the farm was theirs and were even now travelling to find her as they knew she was living with her cousin in Delle. The farmer had been forced into giving them an address and explained in his letter how he was of the opinion that they should expect a visit from Celine soon. He went on to say how there was a party of three men and their ladies intent on taking over the farm immediately under the management of Celine. During the discussion with the farmer two large dogs belonging to Celine became disturbed and seemed intent on barking at the slurry tank.

'Jack' was disappointed that Albert had not been able to make direct contact with his family but was happy that he had been able to find out some details about them. 'Unfortunately, your father had been called up by the German Army,' Albert explained, 'and with very little training was sent to the Meuse Argonne Forest to defend some captured American troops. He was on duty during a diversionary field gun attack by the Americans on some building housing the prisoners when he was killed in the mayhem of trying to escape between the artillery fire and the escaping prisoners. That was the news I managed to learn from a colleague of your father, who was with him at the time. Your mother and sisters were caught up in the confusion at the end of the war and, as the three of them are not German by birth, they are being held at a transit camp intended for prisoner exchange organised through the Swiss Red Cross. The exchange may take some time, but they are safe.

On his return from Strasbourg, Albert drove Else the short journey to the Swiss border. Leaving Else at the border post, he parked his vehicle while she travelled the short distance to her village by a horse and carriage taxi. She quickly sorted her business out with the bank and after a brief visit to a close friend, to tell of her news about Fred, she made her way back to the border where Albert was sleeping in his vehicle. During the journey back to Delle, Albert told Else about the letter addressed to Yvette that Sonia had opened the previous day.

The farmer had been 'strongly' encouraged to give the whereabouts of Yvette. In his letter, he apologised for this and warned that Yvette should expect visitors soon.

CHAPTER 22:
HERBERT SMITH

Herbert Smith and his wife had left England and returned to Paris where a meeting had been arranged with the recently elected ambassador to New Zealand.

Herbert went over the information he had gathered regarding Jack Jackson and expressed his wish to identify the body of the sergeant so his body could be transferred to Canterbury and be re-interred under the memorial to the fallen which was being constructed in the city centre.

A meeting between the NZ ambassador and the French war minister was arranged to reiterate the importance of finding the body of Jack Jackson and to establish whether the information found under the heading 'The Naked Soldier' could in fact be referring to Jack Jackson and, if it was, then they needed to know where was he buried.

The war department carried out a thorough investigation, the result of which placed the naked soldier at an attack on the 29 September 1918 on a German machine gun position, which was responsible for killing and maiming over 250 soldiers. Six brave Allied soldiers had silenced the guns and allowed the army to penetrate German lines.

If the army hierarchy had been more coordinated, then this action would have ended the war within two days and saved tens of thousands of lives. To pacify the NZ ambassador, the French Army joined forces with the French police to investigate a way of confirming the identity of the naked soldier and worked together to find someone who could solve the problem.

The police HQ in Paris messaged each of the 101 departments to ask them to be aware of anyone passing themselves off as an Allied soldier who may possibly be a deserter from the activity during the last month of the war. The message was associated with the actions of the British soldiers drinking in the bar in Paris that had occurred just after hostilities ceased. The local police were aware that those responsible for the events in Paris, and others involved in incidents that had also come to light, had been court martialled and in several cases a guilty verdict had left those involved under the threat of being shot at dawn, so bringing disgrace onto their families.

CHAPTER 23:
THE SEARCH FOR DESERTERS

Else felt threatened by the news from the farmer and decided that she would discuss it with the police sergeant. Else related everything Fred had told her concerning his war service: the meeting with Fritz in a shell hole, the taking of the uniform and identity of a dead soldier, the capture by German forces, the escape and then how they went on to serve the war effort by rescuing trapped US soldiers followed by time spent training new recruits on search and rescue techniques. Else went on to explain how the change in attitude towards them in the village had been stoked up by Artur, the shopkeeper, and had resulted in Yvette and 'Jack' leaving to find work in the new French areas on the Rhine.

The sergeant listened with interest to the story Else was telling him and decided to make his own private notes rather than enter the details of the meeting into the official log book. He planned to write up the official record later.

'I'll be frank with you,' the officer told Else. 'Two days ago, I received from department HQ, a copy of a communication that has been sent to all police stations in France to the effect that anyone suspected of having left their units without written permission, for whatever reason, will be subject to an investigation and a possible court martial. Your Fred and his friend have shown outstanding bravery, but their actions could be interpreted by the recent instruction from department HQ that they left their post and instead of finding their unit, they deserted from the action. I find Fred's story relating to the capture by German soldiers strange and do not understand why your friend "Jack" did not re-join his people, although that may have been considered most unusual with him being in an Allied uniform. That would be hard to explain. Off the record, Else, I should be following up on a claim by one of our villagers, namely Artur, that he has sufficient proof of there being deserters in the village. I have had to officially follow up on this and to satisfy him have arranged a meeting in two days' time. That gives you the rest of the day and all tomorrow to leave the village. I suggest that you both leave as soon as possible and travel to Paris. I will contact the US embassy and arrange for you to meet with General Johnson, who I believe is well known to Fred through his exploits in the Meuse Argonne rescue mission and Fred can himself relay the whole story to him. Earlier today I contacted the US embassy myself and asked to be put through to General Johnson with whom I spoke briefly. I have to say, when I mentioned Fred's name, not only did he remember him, he told me that he had been trying to find him to inform him of a generous financial gesture from the extremely wealthy Van de Veldt family as a reward for helping in the rescue of his only son back in October 1918. You will be made extremely welcome and no doubt the general will offer all necessary help in order to clear Fred's name.'

As the meeting concluded the sergeant told Else that it was quite a story with an amazing sequence of events but that he found her friend Jack's role in the war effort strange.

'Is he German, is he a New Zealander, is he French, is he now American, or is he English?' the sergeant pondered.

'I think he is a bit of each,' was the only answer Else could come up with.

'Don't forget, Else,' the sergeant reassured, 'that if you're in trouble you can rely on me. I will stand by you.'

Else was grateful for the advice from the police sergeant and took full note of what he had said.

Back at Sonia's house, Else told Fred of the outcome of the meeting and their need to leave. During the evening meal the two couples discussed the recent events and how it had ruined the peaceful life they had all enjoyed up until the last few days. Albert offered his suggestion.

'Taking account of the advice from the sergeant and the knowledge that Celine and her Basque friends are likely to visit us soon, I think that it would be advisable for all four of us to leave. I can take the opportunity to arrange a visit to the new Peugeot showroom in the centre of Paris were I have some business matters to discuss. We could drive to Paris, stopping overnight to break the journey. It would give you two a bit of time to consider all your options, although meeting with the senior American officer seems to offer a positive solution.'

CHAPTER 24:
PARIS

The drive through France was very enjoyable and, not feeling the need to rush, they made stops and detours on their way to Paris. The highlight of the journey was a visit to the Chateau du Chenonceau: a beautiful castle built in 1514 spanning the River Cher, which flowed majestically through four bridge arches. Many thought it to be one of the most attractive buildings in the world and a must see for anyone travelling in the Loire area of France.

An overnight stay at Saumur prepared them for the final leg of the journey to Paris. None of the party had visited Paris before so they looked forward to visiting the famous sites. Albert planned to start with the Eiffel Tower, then the museums, the art galleries and, finally, the monuments dedicated to leaders and artists from the past.

Sonia had come up with a different plan. She was happy with the climb up Eiffel Tower but decided that a trip down the Seine followed by a light lunch at the Ritz was preferable to Albert's plans. After lunch Sonia suggested a trip to visit Madame Fol, the favoured dressmaker of the Parisian society whose designs, individuality and quality standard were the envy of all her so-called competitors and Albert would need to be on hand should an article of clothing attract the attention of the ladies.

Staying at the Hotel Westminster, near to La Madeleine, they were within easy walking distance of the US embassy. Sonia and

Else walked the short journey to arrange an appointment with General Johnson, while Albert introduced Fred to a vintage bottle of Meursault, a fine white wine from the Burgundy Region

The general emerged from his office to meet and greet the ladies offering to take the party out the next evening to his favourite restaurant on Rue de Ponthieu.

General Johnson felt it would be more conducive to an open and friendly meeting if they were in a restaurant without the stuffiness of the embassy rooms, especially as a disproportionate number of British officers and minor personnel from the upper crust of British society had an unhealthy interest in all the ins and outs of the US embassy.

'I'm afraid,' the general remarked the next evening, 'that we are still treated as colonials by these people and they fail to realise that if it were not for US intervention in the war, even though it was deemed "last minute when it was virtually over", we would almost certainly be sitting in a province of the German Empire now eating sausages and sauerkraut.'

The general had read the sanitised notes from the police sergeant with great interest

'I have some good news about the naked soldier,' he began 'We are certain that he was buried in the cathedral graveyard in Perone with the inscription on the gravestone: "Here lies a fallen soldier whose name is known only to God". The NZ ambassador is breathing down our necks as they claim the body is that of Jack Jackson of the NZEF: that same Jack Jackson was the brave hero who carried out the rescue of US troops in the Argonne Forest in early October, which means that the 'Jack Jackson' Fred was fighting with must have taken this soldiers clothes and identity. The body could not be identified because of severe facial injuries, so it cannot be proved to the complete satisfaction of the NZ government that we have the right name for the body lying in the cathedral graveyard in Perone.'

Fred said nothing to add to or contradict what the general had said.

'Let me put you in the picture, Fred,' the general continued. 'Under the current witch-hunt for deserters, I am formally obliged to inform the British high commissioner that you are possibly wanted for desertion from the British Army. This I will do tomorrow, but in the meantime, if you look over to the bar there is a gentleman who would like to meet you and introduce himself.' A very smart middle-aged man smiled at the party and came over to the table where an additional place setting was quickly arranged.

'You will have no idea who I am,' the gentleman began as he took his place at the table allowing the ladies to take their seat first. 'I am Joseph Van de Veldt.' He then stood up and shook the hand of each of the party. 'Mr Fred Mills, you do not know what a honour it is to meet you: to meet the man who, along with your colleague, saved the life of my only son after he had been captured by the German army. He had been treated very badly, had gone without food for five days and had little access to clean drinking water. My son would not have survived another day in that hell hole and without my son, my life would not have been worth living, regardless of the tens of millions of dollars in my bank account. I stand here, humbled by your bravery, your skills and your lack of care for the safety of yourself and the same goes for your colleague. The general has given me the details of your incredible journey and I realise that you are in a bit of a pickle. Before we start the meal, here is what we can do. I have taken the opportunity of renting, indefinitely, one of the apartments two blocks down from this hotel that is owned by the US government. I hope you will stay until, together, we can sort out this unfortunate business. So that, Mr Fred Mills, is what we have on the table. Now, let's order some delicious food and some fine wine. General, over to you.'

The American gentleman went on to describe the 'apartment'.

'It has been luxuriously decorated in the latest Parisian fashion and there is a large garden at the rear, for your exclusive use. You will have a small US-born staff to look after your safety, your cleaning, your cooking and your relaxation. I have engaged the top legal brains: experts in defending the innocent who get caught up in this witch-hunt for so called deserters. The senior army prosecutor has had many years' experience in this field so he will be no push-over. But what he doesn't have, however, is the "balls" to do what you and your colleague did. The nearest he would have got to the front line would have been be a wine and lobster event in Deauville.'

Joe Van de Veldt advised the couple with regard to the arrangements he had made.

'With your agreement, after we leave this restaurant, you will be taken to the apartment where your clothes and personal effects have already been attended to. Please bear in mind that the French would not dare attempt to seek you out and the British have no jurisdiction in and around property owned by the US government and the British would not have the mettle to mess with the Van de Veldt family.'

At the end of the meal the party said their goodnights then Fred and Else retired to their new home, or what was to be their home at least for the foreseeable future.

Albert and Sonia spent the night at the Hotel Westminster and the next morning, on checking out, they were pleasantly surprised to find that their bill had already been paid. The couple were met in the foyer of the hotel by an officer of Mr Van de Veldt's company who escorted them the short distance to the US apartment where they said their goodbye's to Fred and Else. Albert and Sonia then they began the long journey home with Sonia looking forward to going back to the quiet life that they had previously enjoyed before the arrival of 'Jack', Yvette, Fred and Else and the distractions from the lady, Celine.

Albert had other plans. During his time in Paris he had formalised a transaction for the sale of his business to a forward looking company who saw the great potential in the future of the motor car.

The motor car was currently only available to the rich who could afford to purchase the car and who could, in most cases, afford to pay the wages of a driver and mechanic. The meeting had been the culmination of intense negotiations between the parties and Albert, with the aid of his accountant, had struck a very lucrative deal which kept a small percentage of the shares to maintain his involvement in the future of the automobile.

Sonia was happy that the burden of running his business was to be taken away from Albert and when he explained his plans for their future she was overjoyed.

Albert had put a deposit on a villa on the shores of Lake Maggiore which would be reserved for the period during the negotiations for the sale of his business. Albert had a copy of the sale brochure which he presented to his wife who immediately fell in love with the villa, but would be sad to move away from Delle, where she had spent all her life to date.

CHAPTER 25:
WASTED JOURNEY

The village square in Delle was a hive of activity with food stalls selling the local liqueur, cheese, butter, a full range of raw meats, an attractive selection of cold cured meats, gherkins, pickled onions and spicy sauces to name but a few. The previous night, Celine and her minders had stayed in a flea pit of a hotel which had left them itching all over. Celine had decided to visit Yvette in Delle to reiterate that the farm in Flavigny belonged to her, not Yvette, and that she would then ensure that her former sister-in-law was 'encouraged' to complete the legal transfer of the farm, and that would be an end to the matter.

On arriving at the village, Celine walked through the stalls taking interest in what was being offered by the stallholders. Her minders went to the busiest bar on the square to have a drink and seek out some local news relating to the Yvette and her friends. The men had been looking forward to having a good drinking session before they started the formal business of persuading Yvette that they meant business and that all she had to do was to sign a pre-prepared document handing the farm over to Celine.

As was the norm, particularly on market day, the wise and the ignorant congregated in one of the local bars to talk, socialise and generally put right all the wrongs of the world. The leader of the pack was Artur, who held court, as was his right, as he owned the biggest business in the village. Artur looked on the group of men sat at the front of the bar with suspicion. He took it on himself to greet the men and ask if they had found the local liqueur to their liking. The response was just a slight smile; it was a brush off and the rest of the locals laughed at Artur. After consuming his first bottle of spirit, one of the visitors asked of the inquisitive man if he knew the whereabouts of a lady called Yvette, who was living on a local farm. Artur composed himself and informed the visitor that she had recently left with her foreign boyfriend, that he believed that they had gone to seek their fortune in the new French lands over towards the Rhine. They had been staying with the automobile man, Albert and his wife, who according to one of his farm workers, had recently taken a trip to Paris to look at the latest models of the 'motor car.'

Artur's drinking partner carried on the story.

'The English soldier and his girlfriend, Else, have gone with them much to the disappointment of Artur here.' He smiled and pointed to the man sat next to him. 'My friend thought he had a chance with her, but he has had his nose pushed out by the English deserter.'

Celine and her group had come a long way on a wasted journey but her men at least found solace in the local spirit.

On arriving back in Delle after the trip to Paris, Sonia was shocked to receive a telegram from the farmer who had rented Yvette's farm. He had been 'encouraged' to hand over the property to Yvette's sister-in-law, Celine, and her male companion along with a small team of experienced farmers from the south west of France.

The neighbour had been informed by one of his workers, who had been busy in the fields next to Yvette's farm, that human remains had been found while cleaning out the blocked slurry tank. The neighbour was surprised that there appeared to be no police involvement and with Celine not having been seen in the town on market day for quite a while, he suspected that the body in the slurry might have been that of her husband who had disappeared some years ago.

The neighbour realised that it was probably best to keep any knowledge regarding Celine to himself, if he knew what was good for him. The Basque people had ways of dealing with problems without interference from the police or any authorities.

Sonia, who initially had mixed feelings about leaving Delle for the villa on the lake soon realised that it was time to move away from the problems brought on them by their friends

CHAPTER 26:
JOSEPH VAN DE VELDT

After giving Fred and Else some time to acclimatise to their new surroundings, the general visited Fred to confirm that he would now have to inform the British embassy that Private Fred Mills of the DCLI, had been reported by a member of the public from the village Delle, in the Department of Territoire de Belfort on the French/Swiss border, and that there was sufficient evidence to investigate this British soldier for desertion.

Mr Van de Veldt had arranged, through his wide range of contacts, to hire a recently retired colonel, Frederick Watson-Hill, as the defence lawyer: an expert in military law, who had sat in on many court martials relating to alleged acts of desertion, cowardice, fraternising with the enemy and other serious charges relating to the recent war. His experience had given him great sympathy for the many soldiers who had been charged with so-called cowardice and was a key figure in re-educating the world so they could understand that many soldiers were suffering from 'shell shock', a traumatic condition caused by war. The army hierarchy had become concerned that too many charges of 'cowardice' had been considered 'not proven' thanks to the influence of the colonel.

A brief, initial meeting had been arranged for early the following week. Fred was interviewed by the colonel under the watchful eye of Ronald Dewhurst III, one of Mr Van de Veldt's senior main

board executives. The meeting lasted for two hours with the agenda covering just five items.
1. The reporting of Fred to the British Army and their response
2. The army and press reporting and the effect it might have on Fred's family
3. Confirmation of the interest shown in the case by the NZ government
4. A brief outline of Fred's actions and details from the morning of the 29 September to the present day
5. The strengths and weaknesses of Fred's defence

The colonel offered no comments but kept notes on everything that was said in the meeting.

Ron Dewhirst summed up by saying that no actions would be taken until a formal response was given directly from the British Army. Ron confirmed that sometime in the near future he would visit the site of the action along with the colonel, a photographer, a member of the Commonwealth War Graves Commission (WGC) familiar with the area of the attack on the Hindenburg Line during the 29 and 30 September 1918 and finally, a soldier who was involved in the action on or around the two days in question.

It took all the Van de Veldt's considerable resources to trace, find and enlist the member of the WGC and a soldier who had been involved in the action.

Unfortunately, the promise of a land fit for heroes never materialised and many of these brave men, who fought not just for the liberty of their own country but for the countries of their allies, found themselves on the scrap heap.

It seemed to be that the winner was in fact the loser and the promise of jobs false, as many men were informed that times were changing.

In reality, the economy was building up to near collapse, something the clever talkers on the wireless had said would be more likely to happen during the mid-1920s.

An advertisement was put in the Manchester Guardian offering three nights in the Somme area of Northern France with extra days each way for travelling and the possibility of a two night stay in Paris. The object of the trip was to collate information regarding the retreat of the German army during the last six weeks of action. The investigation would be demanding and not a holiday. As such there would be complete re-imbursement of any loss of earnings, payment of expenses and a salary of £20.00 per day while away from home. It was a trip solely for soldiers who had seen action during that time and, if interested, should contact the address given with details of their personal involvement in the push to the Hindenburg Line.

Any application was to be submitted to a Miss Gill Goodwin, private secretary to Mr R Dewhurst III. She had worked for the Van de Veldt family for twenty years since the age of fifteen and was very influential. In fact, many thought that she was the brain behind certain commercial aspects of the VdV organisation.

Miss Goodwin expected at least twenty, and possibly up to fifty answers to the advertisement but, in fact, received over two hundred letters, all of them stating that they had been in the area of interest on the dates in question. Through no fault of their own, many returning soldiers had found themselves entrenched in poverty and the thought of having a week away was very attractive. It would mean time to themselves away from nagging wives, screaming children and the embarrassment of having to live off charity or having to ask family, friends and neighbours for a little help. These once proud men who had fought for the liberty of their country and the liberty of their allies were now reduced to begging to survive.

Miss Goodwin, who had reached her position in the VdV

Company through dedication, hard work and being available at the drop of a hat was reduced to tears as she read some of the letters. Most of them had been fighting in either a different area or in reserve trenches that came into action later. But all of them had served in or around the dates in question. After a considerable amount of work, she selected the names of two soldiers who had been in the area of action on the dates in question.

Mr Van de Veldt arrived in the office to discuss the selection for the visit to France with both Miss Goodwin and Ron Dewhirst. Ron had liaised with the WGC and he had been given the name of the charge hand of the BRU, who had discovered the naked soldier and had formally dealt with the paperwork relating to his body. Ron Dewhirst contacted Joe Riley, who immediately agreed to help with the investigation into the actions of Private Fred Mills and to establish whether a charge of desertion could be upheld. The interests of the New Zealand people, who wanted a definite identification of the naked soldier so a ceremonial burial could go ahead, had also to be considered.

At the meeting with Mr Van de Veldt, Miss Goodwin suggested that they take both soldiers to France along with the Mr Joe Riley but also suggested that some assistance be offered to those ex-soldiers who had taken the trouble to write to her offering their services in France.

The suggestion was agreed upon and arrangements were made for staff of the VdV organisation to visit each man who had responded to the advertisement and to offer some financial assistance based on individual needs.

Although the war had ended three years before there remained pressure on the government to step up the search for possible deserters. A group of women who had lost sons in the war, a group who titled themselves 'Mothers of the Fallen', had become more and more vocal in their need for retribution, particularly after the successful court martial of members of the group involved in the Parisian nightclub affair.

Some of the women wanted capital punishment to be meted out to those involved in the Paris affair. This caused a split. While one group insisted that those found guilty should be shot at dawn, a substantial minority called for a guilty verdict, but one that fell short of the ultimate punishment.

CHAPTER 27:
THE CHARGES AGAINST PRIVATE FRED MILLS

The search for deserters found nearly fifty soldiers who had left the army under a variety of circumstances. One of the main reasons for 'desertion' involved choosing the warm bed of a French lover rather than sleeping on the cold and damp floor in a tented village, initially erected as a holding camp while soldiers were dismissed from service and transport home organised. There was near mutiny when it was announced that those soldiers last to arrive at the front had been the given priority to be sent home over those who, in some cases, had served for four years. The reasoning behind this unpopular action was given that the men called up last could more easily fit back into lives and jobs back home.

Pressure for increased numbers of court martials grew resulting in severe delays and a backlog of six months became the norm. When the case of Private Fred Mills entered the case log, it presented a diversion from the more routine cases the courts generally had to deal with. Fred's was an interesting but complicated case that had been reported by the Americans with the accused private staying in a luxurious apartment owned by the American embassy. It was a case the most experienced members of the army hierarchy wanted to get their teeth into so they could let their cousins from across the Atlantic know who was running the show. Top army officers had the opinion of 'Thanks for your help towards the end of the conflict, but we can carry on without you now.' Cheerio, and goodbye was the watchword. 'Leave it to us now. Yanks go home!'

The waiting time for run of the mill cases was getting on for six months but the case against Fred Mills was to be started in approx. three months. As the charge sheet was being written the list of charges became longer.

1. Cowardice
2. Desertion
3. Treason

The British Army initially demanded that Private Mills be tried in London. Under some technicality the American government and the New Zealand parliament gave grounds for the trial to be held elsewhere, so there could be impartial judgement. The British government, through the army leadership, could not be seen to offer leniency in dealing with the cases being put before them, whereas the US and NZ governments demanded that fair and reasonable treatment be offered to Private Fred Mills and to that end it was reluctantly agreed by the British that the case be dealt with on French soil.

The questions to be answered were as follows:

Did Private Fred Mills desert his duty on the 29 September 1918?

It was unlikely that the British Army prosecution would be interested in the actions relating to a NZ soldier who had been left naked in the ground: nor would they be interested in any alleged deeds of extreme heroism that this same soldier may or may not have carried out.

Did he desert his post? Yes or no!

Through the influence of the Van de Veldt organisation and to guard American interest in the outcome of actions against US soldiers who fought in France, a senior officer was to be made available to represent the United States. The head of forces in Europe, General John Pershing, brought together the leadership who still had duties and commitments in France and outlined the British Army case against Fred Mills. At a meeting held in the US embassy in Paris the draft of charges and actions likely to be levelled against Private Mills was discussed. It was unanimously agreed that this brave soldier must be protected against the too often insane actions meted out against young men who fought for their country and who, for just one moment in the heat of battle, lost the ability to fight. It was agreed that General Johnson, who had direct knowledge relating to the actions of Private Mills, be put in overall charge of the wellbeing of this soldier. The general would be given any resources that he may need.

One aspect of the defence requiring great sensitivity was the contact with Fred's family back in Lancashire. This had to be handled very carefully because, after the euphoria of discovering her son, who had been deemed 'killed in action' was alive, his family would then be faced with the 'Mothers of the Fallen,' who would make loud demands to politicians and well-known public figures for Fred to face 'justice'.

A discussion between Ron Dewhirst and Gill Goodwin ensued and several options for breaking the news to Fred Mills' mother were put forward. Whichever option they chose, the news had to be delivered very carefully. They decided that it would be best for Miss Goodwin to liaise with members of VdV who were delivering on the promise to reward those who had answered the advertisement for the trip to France. Having checked there were at least seven of the ex-soldiers within a two mile radius of the Mills' home in Kempsey Street with one on Queen Street which ran adjacent to the Mills' home, Gill Goodwin decided to take personal responsibility for delivering parcels to the seven houses in the locality of the Mills' household.

News of those who were to be given rewards spread like wildfire and, without doubt, Fred's mother would have been made aware of this act of generosity, so, would not be too surprised if someone turned up at her door. It would then be a case of Gill breaking the news to her about Fred.

It was Fred's youngest brother, George, named after his cousin, who ran to his mother with the news that a posh lady had delivered a parcel to a house on Queen Street and was asking where Kempsey Street was.

'I think, Mother, that she has something to do with the war.'

'George, you better make yourself scarce if she's coming here,' his mother replied. 'I haven't a clue what it could be about. It might be something good or it could be something bad and we've had enough bad news with our Fred being killed and your father out of work.'

'Mrs Mills?' The lady at the door smiled. 'My name is Gill Goodwin. I work for a very wealthy American company and I have some news to give you. Can we go inside and discuss the matter privately?' The two women went inside where Mary Anne insisted on making a cup of tea for them both. 'There's nothing that's so important it can't wait for a kettle to boil now is there, miss?' she proffered after going through the ritual of brewing the pot of tea and getting out the best china. 'Now what's all this about?' Mary Anne asked. 'What brings a posh lady like you to Kempsey Street. You'll need to get to the point as I'm on tenterhooks here.'

Gill changed her smile to a more serious expression. 'It's about your son. Fred.'

'Well Fred can't have done anything,' Mary Anne interrupted. 'he was killed at the end of September just before the war ended.'

Gill shook her head. 'No. That's not what happened. He didn't die as the records show. He became disorientated and finished up fighting for the Americans alongside a friend from New Zealand.

More to the point they carried out an extreme act of bravery and rescued many American soldiers who were being held under terrible conditions. One of those soldiers was the only son of my boss, Mr Van de Veldt, who is an extremely wealthy American billionaire and wants to reward the great work of your Fred and his friend by helping out both families.'

Mary Anne nearly fainted as she shouted for George to go and get Alice, her sister-n-law, from next door, to come in and listen to some news. As it happened, Alice had put a glass to the wall and had been trying her best to listen in to what was being said anyway. After she had made a more official entrance, Mary Anne told her that Fred was still alive and, after that, the two women bombarded Gill Goodwin with questions:

'So what happens next?'

'When is our Fred coming home?'

'He's not badly injured or anything is he?'

'Why didn't he write to us to let us know where he is?'

Mary Anne had a dozen questions to ask and Alice chipped in with a few herself.

Gill went on to explain the situation regarding Fred. 'He is likely to be charged with desertion by the British Army, which is completely untrue as he in no way deserted but re-joined the fighting as soon as possible. He has the full weight of one of the richest men in America behind him. One hundred percent.'

Miss Goodwin went on to explain that the news regarding Fred would soon be made public and inevitably there would be a backlash by people who were not privy to the facts, the most vocal of these being 'Mothers of the Fallen'.

'We will ensure that the reports of Fred's bravery is prioritised and we will have a large legal company based in Manchester, on call, and at your disposal at any time day or night. Like I explained before,

Mr Van de Veldt has given Fred's situation his full backing along with all the resources the VdV organisation has available. I will leave now, but before I go here is a small parcel for you from my boss.' With that Miss Goodwin left the two ladies to take in what had just happened.

CHAPTER 28:
REVISITING THE BATTLE SITE

The two selected soldiers soon discovered that the trip to the scene of the Battle for the Hindenburg Line was by no means a 'jolly.' The soldiers met up at a pre-booked hotel in the centre of Manchester having travelled from Accrington and Wigan respectively. Early in the morning they met up with Joe Riley, who lived just outside Manchester, a twenty minute ride on the number 82 tram. The three had second-class tickets to London which allowed them a seat in a partitioned carriage. That same day a huge crowd of football fans were making their way to London to support Bolton Wanderers who were due to play West Ham United at the newly completed Wembley Stadium. The station was packed to capacity and the three men could barely make it through the crowds of fans who were all trying to squeeze themselves on the next train south. Eventually, having got on the designated train they made their way to the allocated compartment where a burly man in his twenties had his foot jammed against the door so no one could get in to disturb him and his five Bolton fans. As a result, the three men spent the whole of the five hour journey stood up in the heat of the day breathing in the sweat of the fans and the smell of piss from men relieving themselves where they stood. It was a great start to the 'adventure in France'!

Once they arrived in London they met up with the defence lawyer, Frederick Watson-Hill, together with Ron Dewhirst and Gill

Goodwin, who was to be the photographer.

The train to Dover was pleasant enough, but the sea crossing from Dover to Le Havre was extremely rough. All suffered with seasickness and were glad to reach land safely. A combination of the train journey and sea crossing left them smelly, wet and disorientated so Ron decided that they had better find a hotel in town. The only hotel available had just four rooms available so there was no choice but to share as best they could. It was late the following evening when they reached Perone, where they were to stay for three nights. After the evening meal, Mr Watson-Hill set out what he needed to see during the ensuing two days when they visited the area where his client had allegedly deserted.

The plan of activity centred on these questions:
1. Where did Fred and his colleagues stay on the two nights before the action on 29 September?
2. What were the objectives for the following days?
3. Who was the senior officer controlling the planned attack?
4. Who was giving the orders for the plan of attack?
5. What time was the first wave planned to move forward?
6. Each soldier to describe the events from the order to advance.
7. Did either soldier have direct knowledge of Fred Mills?
8. Did either soldier have any knowledge at all of Fred Mills?
9. Did either soldier have knowledge of the attack on the machine gun by NZ troops?
10. Fred Mills has been accused of desertion and cowardice. What is your opinion of that?

At the end of the two days the team would come to know Fred's character inside out. The defence lawyer would have meetings with ex-colleagues from the DCLI and from other regiments to discuss the facts relating to Fred Mills and gauge the strength of the case for his defence.

CHAPTER 29:
PREPARATION FOR THE COURT MARTIAL

On returning to Paris, the defence lawyer met with General Johnson to go through and analyse the results from the visit to Perone. It seemed that there were more questions than answers arising from the visit to the site of the battles on and around the 29 September 1918. The area of the battle for La Vacquerie was still a churned up quagmire and the sight of military cemeteries between St Quentin, Perone and the Somme had driven home the scale of the carnage between 1914 and 1918.

Anticipating a close fought battle between the prosecution and the defence, Ron Dewhirst sourced two additional clerks with court room experience to present the information pertaining to Fred Mills in a clear, concise and articulate manner.

The DL was spending a significant amount of his time debating with the British Army as to the location of the court martial. There was much to take into account as all four parties had particular interest in the case. Obviously there was France, where the action had taken place; Britain, Fred's homeland and the country for whom he fought; the United States, whose wish was to present Fred with their highest award for bravery; finally, there was New Zealand, whose dead soldier's identity was used to disguise the true identity of an enemy soldier.

Several possible options were submitted. The British Army

expressed their wish that they wanted the court martial to be held on home soil as it was a British soldier that was involved. The other three parties were against this option. Each having their own reasons. A solution was put forward by the defence lawyer was to re-open the former British Army GHQ at Montreuil-sur-Mer, which had been closed in 1919 and was currently being used as a military academy. These buildings had the benefit of relative isolation while being easily accessible from both London and Paris. The British Army agreed to the choice of venue and a time limit of ten weeks for both parties to prepare for the proceedings was agreed, with the court martial being set to take place four weeks after that. This would allow time for both the prosecution and defence teams to bring witnesses to the table. The location also had the benefit of being close to plenty of hotels, some excellent, which would cater for all levels of comfort and sophistication. The legal staff, witnesses, public and the press would all find something to their taste. The press interest had started to grow once the dates had been agreed and it didn't take long before the Manchester newspapers had got hold of the story and descended on Kempsey Street to try and expand on what was already known about Fred Mills and the actions he had been involved in.

As the location of the trial in France became public, 'The Mothers of the Fallen' turned up in significant numbers although the VdV organisation was on hand to keep the MOTF in check, at least for the time being. Every hint of cowardice was to be countered with an action of Fred Mill's that emphasised his bravery. The mention of desertion would be rounded on with the dates of the action that resulted in the rescue the trapped US troops. Also, how could you desert for four days in a complicated field of action over a five hundred kilometre long front line, stretching from the North Sea to Switzerland?

To keep a close eye on every detail of the trial, the US government had taken a six-month lease on Beaurepaire, a country house that had been the residence of Sir John Haig, commander-in-chief during the war. It was agreed by the defence that Fred and Else were to stay at Beaurepaire for the duration of the court martial under the protection of the US government and the VdV organisation.

CHAPTER 30:
THE COURT MARTIAL – PROSECUTION

The 'overseas' court martial convened and was to be overseen by a tribunal consisting of four commissioned officers and a 'judge advocate' who would controlled the proceedings. After all charges had been presented and the defence against those charges laid out, the judge advocate, with help from the four other judges, would pass sentence and he alone would decide on the level of punishment.

The prosecutor and his team were to open the case against Fred Mills and to set out clearly and concisely the charges against him, present the evidence and summon witnesses for the five officials to consider. Once the prosecutor had made his case, the defence team was to answer any charges against the accused, summon witnesses to contradict the accusations and offer any relevant information to substantiate a counter argument.

The first day of the court martial became a media circus with reporters present from each of the four countries directly involved, plus a team from Denmark, who had been approached by a consortium of the German press to report on any involvement concerning the Weimar Republic of Germany, the designated title of the German state since 1918. The presence of the 'Mothers of the Fallen' was represented by six women who had arrived via the Dover to Boulogne Ferry and were staying in private accommodation in nearby La Touquet, where a large contingent of ladies were planning to make their feelings known to all by gathering at the military academy gates.

While the press and public were not allowed in a private military court, it had been agreed that they would be given a reasonably detailed statement at the end of each day's proceedings by a court clerk.

The prosecution's presentation commenced on the Tuesday and was led by James Grant KC, who had trained as a barrister before the outbreak of the war and had joined up as an officer straight away. Through his leadership skills and steadfastness under enemy fire he had attained the rank of colonel. The defence lawyer, Mr Watson-Hill, recognised James Grant as a formidable opponent who would seriously challenge his abilities during the court martial.

James Grant stood up, faced the accused first and then turned to the panel of four officers with the judge advocate sitting between them. James Grant addressed Private Mills directly. 'I stand here as the representative of the Crown, His Majesty King George V, and my duty is to determine whether a member of the armed forces is guilty of an action, or actions, that are listed in the Army Schedule of Offences. If anyone is found guilty of any these offences that are listed, a choice of punishments will be considered that are appropriate to the severity of the offences committed. Having said that if, within the duration of the court martial, I find that the charges made against the accused person do not appear to have substance, then I will recommend that the action be closed and the accused person be allowed to walk free without any blemish on his record. Private Fred Mills, do you understand what has been said?'

Fred replied to affirm that he fully understood the charges laid against him.

The prosecution opened up by asking Fred Mills to confirm his identity.

'Fred Mills, private, Duke of Cornwall's Light Infantry, 30103, sir.'

'And when did you enlist, Private Mills?'

'First of August 1916.'

'Were you called up or did you volunteer?'

'I was called up, but I was going to volunteer in September, sir'

'So you were called up and you did not volunteer?'

'Yes, sir.'

'We will focus on events that took place at the end of September 1918. So you spent just over two years as a soldier and no promotion. Any reason why you had been overlooked, Private Mills?'

'Yes sir, there was a reason. It was a mix up between myself, Fred Mills, and my cousin and best friend, George Mills. Both of us were recommended for promotion by Captain Stephen of the DCLI but an apparent error by the battalion clerk resulted in only one of the applications being sanctioned, that of George Mills. Captain Stephen confirmed that the matter would be rectified straight after the push on the Hindenburg Line when we returned to our Barracks. I hope that answers your question, sir'.

'It partly answers my question, but of course you never returned to barracks did you? But we will deal with the reasons for that later.'

'No sir, I never did return back to barracks. That was due to the circumstances I found myself in. But very many of my friends and colleagues did not return back to barracks, as a direct result of the carnage we experienced that day.'

'We will deal with those circumstances later. Private Mills, I have checked on your service history and I find that your records have not been kept up to date. Do you know of any reason why that might be? Also, please tell me what action you did see during your time in France.'

'Firstly, sir, I saw action on the Somme between late Summer of 1916 and early 1917 and then spent the summer of 1917 in Belgium near to Ypres. During the early part of 1918 until that summer I helped to fight off the German offensive and later spent time around Amiens. From June onwards my unit, DCLI prepared for the attack on the H Line, which commenced on the 29 September 1918. Apart for the time that I fought around Amiens, I fought alongside my cousin, George, and other members of what was originally the Oldham Pals. I think, sir, with due respect, that I have seen at least as much action if not more than anyone in this court.'

'Thank you, Private Mills, for enlightening us on your actions. Let me now set out the three actions that you are to be charged with in contravention of the military act.

1. That in the face of the enemy you showed cowardice in that you were seen by members of your battalion to be hiding in a shell hole. In effect you disengaged yourself from the enemy and let down your fellow soldiers, your unit and yourself.

2. After sheltering yourself for a long period of time and possibly (but not proven) pretending to play dead, a concentrated attack on the Germans lines pushed them back and the attacking units moved forward, at which point you deserted your post and instead of trying to find your unit set off in the opposite direction.

3. For reasons we will talk about to later, you colluded with a soldier of the enemy and after finding out that the German soldier spoke passable English, your hatched a plan to hide this German soldier's identity by stealing the uniform off a dead Allied soldier, who is believed to be Sergeant Jack

Jackson from Canterbury New Zealand. He was the same Jack Jackson that led an attack on a German machine gun post, but unfortunately was killed and his face destroyed to make positive identification impossible. I must now tell you that the second in command on that attack was none other than George Mills, your cousin. Because of the actions of yourself and this German soldier a charge of treason is added to the other two charges.

'Private Mills you are to be charged with not one, not two, but three actions in contravention of the military law of the United Kingdom.

'I now ask the judge advocate that proceedings be postponed for today and for the next two days allowing formal documents to be prepared by the Crown and to give the accused, Private Fred Mills, time to discuss these contraventions with his defence team in order to set out some answers to the three charges that I have brought before the proceedings today.'

With that, the judge advocate spoke with his fellow judges and having received confirmation, closed the court for that day and the following two days.

CHAPTER 31:

MOTHERS OF THE FALLEN (MOTF)

Outside the court building there was an atmosphere of excitement upon hearing the charges to be made and the Mothers of the Fallen, now reinforced by locals, were largely happy with the summary of actions from that day.

A meeting was hastily arranged between the defence lawyer, General Johnson, Ronald Dewhirst and Fred Mills with Miss Goodwin taking notes and organising the proceedings.

Ron opened the meeting. 'We seem to be in a bit of a pickle with Colonel James Grant KC giving a very articulate summary of the three charges.'

The defence lawyer agreed. 'He is gently leading the judges down the traditional route of charge, guilty verdict and punishment. That was expected. I would have done the same in his place. He has made it clear that any events after Fred and his colleague left the general battle zone are of no consequence to the charges made by the Crown. In a black and white scenario all three charges could stick, but I am here to not so much disprove the charges but to add circumstances that will muddy the water and throw the charges out. These five judges have got their eye on the race meeting at Chantilly and the prospect of a long weekend without their wives so they will be looking to tie matters up as quickly as possible. Our job is to at least cast doubt on the three charges. I have all the material I need to defend Fred, so please be patient with me and let me do my job.'

The remaining three days were taken up with the defence lawyer and Fred going through different questions that the prosecution might come up with, while Ron took it upon himself to familiarise himself with the members of the MOTF.

His American charm caught the eye of two of the more vivacious members of the group and without being too obvious he conversed easily with some of the younger widows who, with no men around, had used the organisation as a social meeting group.

Ron was careful not to come over as too friendly but the decision to change hotels from Beaurepaire to one of the very pleasant hotels in La Touquet put him closer to the discussions being carried out in a more relaxed atmosphere.

The third day of the court martial carried on in the same vein as day one and part of day two. Fred stood up well against the questions and charges brought by the prosecution: the time spent on discussions in the previous days had certainly paid off. He gave his answers in a clear and concise manner and he avoided the flippant remarks that the prosecution were hoping to extract from him.

Towards the end of the fourth day the defence lawyer asked the judge advocate if he could commence his defence on the Saturday instead of leaving it until the Monday afternoon when the defence was scheduled to begin.

The faces of the four judges all turned to the judge advocate. If granted, this would spoil the planned weekend for the five in Deauville and, as the judge advocate hesitated, the defence lawyer intervened.

'Let me converse with my client and his team to see if we could abandon the idea of the court in session over weekend. Perhaps, we all need the weekend to go through the details of the court martial and a weekend by the sea going over our notes is preferable to getting bogged down in the court. Can I ask you to review the weekend options and let us reconvene at, say, 1 pm on Monday.'

This was accepted and the prosecution soon realised that the defence team's tactic had scored points with the judges.

Ron had pre-empted the weekend break and Miss Goodwin had booked him a sea-view suite in the Hotel Metropole in La Touquet. A Saturday morning stroll on the beach, after eating a hearty breakfast of smoked fish and scrambled eggs, cleared Ron's head and finding an isolated spot amongst the sand dunes he sat down and took out his copy of Les Misérables by Victor Hugo, which was set in nearby Montreuil-sur-Mer. He only got to page 12 before being spotted by Mrs Cynthia Williams, wife of the late Lieutenant Coronel Terence John Williams, known affectionately as TJ to his troops.

TJ Williams had been killed by a stray shell on the 10 November 1918.

Ron's peace was suddenly interrupted.

'I hope you are enjoying your book, Mr Dewhirst, and do forgive my intrusion into your nice little hideaway. I am Cynthia Williams, co-founder and secretary of the Mothers of the Fallen. I have been camped outside the gates of the military academy and I am up to date with all the proceedings. We have not been privy to the actions of Private Mills, only that he deserted his post with a member of the enemy but I am sure that there is more to it than that. Are you able to give more details as to the action of the private? I believe that a certain American billionaire is involved in the case because Fred Mills and another soldier saved the life of many US Soldiers that had been captured and treated appallingly by the German Army. My organisation is never in full knowledge of the facts and we can come across as being a death squad rather than a sympathetic group of widows and mothers. I can assure you, Mr Dewhirst, that the majority of our members are no 'death squad'. Perhaps if you have time, we could meet informally and fill in any gaps so both parties can deal with the truth rather than rumour and guess work. Is that of interest to you, Mr Dewhirst?'

'Yes, that would be fine, and please call me Ron.'

'Agreed, and it's Cynthia. Perhaps we could meet up for lunch somewhere quiet so that we can concentrate on laying down the facts as opposed to making assumptions about Private Mills' actions.'

'That would be fine,' replied Ron. 'I can, if you wish, arrange a lunch in the dining room at my suite in the Metropole. I'm sure that you may wish to bring a colleague so I will arrange a table setting for three.'

Cynthia smiled at the suggestion. 'Ron, I am a bit long in the tooth for a chaperone. I had been married for ten years with three children when TJ was blown to bits. Anyway, this is France and a man with two ladies in his room would be of no matter. A ménage a trois is not uncommon with upper class ladies in France; so you must be careful in your arrangements because the hotel staff might jump to the wrong conclusions.'

Fred and Else had the weekend to review the situation and discuss their future together. Fred had total faith in his defence team, and knew, whatever the verdict, the VdV organisation had its tentacles all over the globe. Fred felt safe and Else was confident that Fred would be found innocent of all charges so they felt it was appropriate to discuss the subject of marriage. They agreed that within a month, after the court martial, they would marry and, if at all possible, would marry in Switzerland.

The weekend was soon over. Ron was happy, Fred was happy and the defence lawyer was brimming with confidence that nothing could go wrong.

CHAPTER 32:
THE COURT MARTIAL – CHARGES AGAINST PRIVATE FRED MILLS

The court martial reconvened at 1:30 pm on Monday, a little later than planned as one of the judges had some last minute business to attend to having miscalculated his expenditure over the weekend and so had to wait until the banks opened to be able to clear his debts.

The prosecution began by reminding the judges of the status of the court martial and the three charges against Private Fred Mills.

James Grant KC started to go through each of the charges starting with desertion. He laid great emphasis on the effect on soldier's morale when someone shirked their responsibilities.

'If every soldier had taken the attitude as Private Fred Mills none of us would be here today. We would have been tortured and shot dead. Anyone left would be speaking German and living in dire conditions. Tens, probably hundreds of thousands of soldiers, like Private Mills, have given up their lives to protect the future for us all: the future of France; the future of our friends across the Atlantic who were good enough to come over to help, albeit at the last minute to get their name on the scoresheet; the future of New Zealand, whose soldiers suffered more losses per population than any other nation; and last, but certainly not least, is the British Armed Forces who came into this war for the sake of little Belgium. I have a report from a junior officer who confirms that he saw Private Mills hiding in a shell hole holding what looked like a satchel, which probably contained the day's plan of action. This junior officer has made a sworn statement to that effect. I put it to you that Private Fred Mills let the side down by hiding in a shell hole instead of advancing and is, therefore, guilty of cowardice.'

A break of thirty minutes was granted to the prosecution in order for Grant and his team to clarify a point of law regarding the distinction between cowardice and desertion.

The case against Private Fred Mills continued on the charge of desertion. James Grant raised his voice. 'Is desertion more serious than cowardice? Maybe it is, perhaps it isn't. Possibly both charges go hand in hand. Does a coward go on to desert his duty, his instructions and his post? Private Mills did all three. Is he therefore three times a coward? Hiding, then running away: deserting. What about his fellow soldiers, what did they do? I'll tell you what they did. They marched across no man's land to take out the enemy. It was kill or be killed. There was no backtracking for these men. They had one aim, one direction and one goal: take out that machine gun nest, fight and kill the enemy in their own trenches whatever the cost. Don't stop to help the soldier who fell in front of you even though it might have been your best friend; it might have been your sergeant. Don't stop to see who it is. Keep moving forward. Take out that machine gun. Push the enemy back a mile, then another mile, then back to where they started from in 1914. No, that's not enough. They wanted our land, now let's take their land. Let's take back the land lost by France in 1871. Let us give the Hun a good beating so that they never attack a neighbouring country again. That is what his fellow soldiers did while Private Fred Mills deserted his post and he is a coward.'

Grant paused for a glass of water then continued.

'Gentlemen, Judges, I have presented not one, but two of the most serious offences that contravene military law. Please bear with me because I have a third to bring to you.

'We are talking about a war that was to be ended by Christmas 1914, a war that became one of attrition. What would the 6 million soldiers, sailors, airmen and all people think when I outline what the third charge is against this so-called soldier?' He pointed to Fred. 'What can possibly be worse than the two other charges we have talked about. What do you think of a soldier who colluded with the enemy? I'm talking about colluding with a German soldier. Does that not make you feel sick in your stomachs? Private Fred Mills tells us that the man he calls Fritz was not German, that he was English. Rubbish! Forget the upbringing in Manchester, forget the English mother: Fritz, or whatever he is called, is, was and always will be German and as evil as any other German. Born in England? Forget it! His first language is English? Forget it. He is a German, and the Germans were our enemy and that is the beginning, the middle and the end of it. Private Fred Mills knowingly colluded with an enemy soldier.'

The defence lawyer was impressed with the prosecution speeches and as the judge advocate brought the day's business to an end he smiled and nodded at his opponent. It had been a job well done: a challenge for the defence team to respond to the next day.

CHAPTER 33:
THE COURT MARTIAL – DEFENCE

The day set off with a more sympathetic mood towards the defendant. The VdV organisation had provided the crowd at the gate with a detailed synopsis of the rescue of the US soldiers trapped and encircled in the Argonne Forest. The rescue was accepted as one of the top ten military actions during WW1 and, to put the rescue in perspective, events had been published in the Boy's Own weekly magazine as a popular, true story that ran for four editions.

The defence lawyer had an air of confidence that he had not shown to date, but Fred was nervous of being interrogated by his own team. The defence team had insisted that Fred should act normally, answer the questions truthfully and stick to the points: no wise comments.

The defence lawyer stood and faced the judges then began his address.

'If I may, can I firstly comment on the prosecution delivery yesterday? Although I will question some and probably most of his statement, I found it to be one of the most clear and concise assessments that I have ever had the pleasure to listen to. The prosecution has given us three charges in contradiction of military law and I intend, with the help of Private Fred Mills, the accused soldier, to answer each one. Dealing with the first charge of cowardice: Private Mills can you tell us what actually happened during the early hours of the action on 29 September 1918?'

'Sir, I wish to make it clear that I am a very experienced soldier, having been on or near the front line for most of the two years that I served the king in France. I saw action and fought the enemy during my time in France in several locations and was directly involved in some major battles. I have already given this court details of service to my country. I would go as far as to say that I have probably seen more front line fighting than all the personnel in this room put together. If you take my service and multiply it by thousands, then that will reflect the level of commitment the average "Tommy" has given to the Allies. On the day in question we had been training for what we had been assured would be the final action of the war and that the Germans would either surrender or start running back to their homes in the Black Forest, in Berlin, in Munich or wherever. We were told before we went over the top that the German defence would be non-existent. This was the mindset that the officers had drilled into us. Our guns fired incessantly. When the whistles blew and we climbed the ladder we were met with an eerie silence as we walked behind the Scottish man playing his bagpipes. For a minute it was as our sergeant had told us it would be: 'a piece of piss'. Then all of a sudden a cacophony of machine gun fire and small arm fire was cutting us down. To cap it all our guns had for some reason changed their aim and shells were exploding behind us as we moved steadily forward in an effort to save our energy for the final push into the German trenches.

'It was carnage. Utter carnage. It was as though the world had come to an end. Judgement day!

'Soldiers I had fought with for two years were falling in front of me, to the side of me and with the shell fire from our own side, to the back of me as well. All I could do was move forward in a steady manner, just hoping and praying that the bullets would miss me, which they did, but out of the corner of my eye I saw Captain Stephen fall: he had been hit. We are told to keep moving forward, but instinct took over and I went to his aid.

'The captain had served the DCLI for the last twelve months and I have had the pleasure of being of service to him, helping him with more mundane duties while he concentrated on the planning and organisation of the soldiers under his command. After he fell, I stopped for a short time to help him and although in great pain, he handed me his satchel that contained the maps and battle plans for the next days. He told me to take the satchel and hand it to one of his fellow officers. I stayed with him for only a few minutes hoping that the medical team would arrive to tend to his wounds. I fully understand that we should move forward at all times, but I could not leave my officer with whom I had served for a year to die on his own in a mud-filled shell hole. I stayed with him until a junior officer arrived, and I handed over the satchel to him. The captain gave me a private message for his fiancée and I left him. At about the same time the Germans had laid the area with mustard gas and smoke screen. So yes, I did become disorientated. I soon teamed up with a squad of Australian soldiers and four of us moved forward together shell hole to shell hole towards the enemy positions. Shortly afterwards a shell exploded to the side of these three soldiers who I had been advancing with men and killed them instantly, having taken the full force of the shell and in doing so protecting me from a similar fate. I was, however, stunned and dazed and I lost my hearing. I must have laid still for quite a while. Eventually I came to my senses and I cautiously raised my body from the wall of the shell hole and started walking in no particular direction. without knowing where I was. Did I desert? Certainly not. Was I a coward? Definitely not.'

'Would a coward have spent two years face to face with the enemy?

'Would a coward have spent weeks fighting an uphill battle at Thiepval on the Somme?

'Might I also ask, what kind of coward fights hand to hand with a bayonet at Amiens?

'So, no sirs, I am not a coward and I didn't desert. I may have walked in circles, but you had to be there to comprehend how hard it was to keep a straight line amongst bursts of machine gun fire combined with the noise of British shells exploding behind you. Then there was the smoke, the gas and the screams of men trapped in barbed wire begging fellow soldiers to put them out of their misery. No sirs, because you were not there then you have no concept of how hard it was to endure the sheer carnage and misery of that day.'

The defence lawyer felt like clapping at such a heart-felt summary of the events on the morning of the 29 September 1918. He turned briefly to face the judges and the look on their faces showed just how moved they were by Private Mills' account. But the judge advocate kept a straight face and maintained a stern look. His mind was fixed on the ultimate penalty for this soldier, who in his mind, was guilty of all three charges and would more than deserve what would hopefully be coming to him.

The defence continued.

'The prosecution spoke of Private Mills allegedly hiding in a shell hole. Well, yes he was in a shell hole; a shell hole with his officer, who was handing over a satchel with maps and battle plans. As the captain was hit he fell onto his satchel and a passing soldier or officer could have misconstrued Private Mills gently lifting the captain's body to retrieve the satchel.

'I have tried, but failed, to identify the passing soldier mentioned by the prosecution. I have, however, successfully located the junior officer mentioned by Private Mills and he has made a statement concerning his memory of that fleeting event. I will pass this to the judge advocate to read and perhaps comment'.

Rather than read it himself the judge advocate passed it to the judge on his left without even a glance at the contents then nodded for the defence to continue.

The judge put on his spectacles and commenced to read out the statement.

'I am George Haig, a retired major: retired due to a serious injury that I suffered on the 29 September 1918. After spending several months in a hospital in Deauville, I was discharged with a pension from the army. I am luckier than most: I survived. That day, the 29 September, was carnage, complete and utter carnage. In the first three hours of that morning in the vicinity of the village of La Vacquerie, I would say that as many of our soldiers were killed by friendly fire as there were killed by the enemy. Whilst I do not use family connections to comment on or discuss the war, I did, in this instance, write to my Uncle John to inform him of the problems that we faced on that day in the hope that lessons could be learnt. He received it, he read it and replied "Thank you, Uncle John".

The defence turned to the judges. 'To summarise, I submit on behalf of Private Fred Mills that the charges listed as one and two on the charge sheet have no substance and should be entered on the record as innocent as opposed to not proven.'

After reading the statement the judge looked at his colleagues. 'I suggest that we take a break from proceedings and reconvene tomorrow at ten.'

All parties were in agreement and the court dispersed. On the way out James Grant KC acknowledged the day's work from the defence team.

CHAPTER 34:
THE COURT MARTIAL – SUMMING UP

The evening meal was eaten individually in their rooms, having first had a couple of drinks in the bar. Fred's defence team knew that the next day was going to be tough as Fred's collusion with the enemy was to be discussed.

Ron Dewhirst stayed behind for another drink before retiring to his suite. As he opened the door he could smell a strong but not unpleasant perfume. He checked to see if he was actually in the right room.

Satisfied that he was actually in his room, he walked through the reception room into his bedroom. His breath was taken from him when he saw Miss Goodwin and Mrs Williams sat up in bed with silk sheets tucked under their chins: Mrs Williams who had told him that he needed to be careful in France!

Everyone had agreed on an early breakfast but Ron had left a message to say that he had gone to interview the spokesperson for the Mothers of the Fallen and had taken Miss Goodwin along to take notes. He had stressed that it was important for the defence team to maintain good relations with the MOTF, whatever the verdict. The spokesperson, Mrs Williams, needed to be convinced that Private Fred Mills was a completely different type of person than the despicable drunks in that Paris night club. Ron had promised the defence lawyer that he would try to get her away from the MOTF group and have a one to one with her to paint a more acceptable picture of Fred. Ron had said it would be hard but he was confident that with the help of Miss Goodwin she would change her position and encourage other members to follow her example.

The defence opened the proceedings with the usual pleasantries and called on Private Fred Mills to explain the events and circumstances relating to his meeting and his then befriending this German soldier known only as Fritz.

Fred looked round the courtroom, knowing that his neck was on the line. He realised that whatever he said, he would not change the attitude of the judge advocate.

He was a man of vast experience who had sat in many court martials, and although he claimed and presented himself as totally unbiased, records showed that all who came before him had been found guilty as charged with only one exception. This was an occasion when he had charged the wrong twin, who had actually been in the mid-Atlantic rather than the Somme from where he was accused of deserting his post on the 1 July 1916. It had taken some months for the judge to recover from the smirks and jokes at his expense.

His career highlight had been judging a sixteen-year-old lad guilty of deserting his post and sentencing him to the firing squad the morning after the trial. This poor young lad had a large quantity of rum forced down him so he had no conception of what was about to happen to him. He died from a single bullet to his heart. The other five soldiers in the firing squad had inexplicably missed the target pinned on his heart.

Fred cleared his throat and commenced.

'Sirs, I have tried to explain the confusion on that day, the 29 September 1918. It was chaos: it was shell fire, it was smoke, it was mustard gas and it was the screams of young men who were little more than boys,

shouting for their mothers. It is difficult to explain disorientation. You have no regard for your own safety. Your life is on the line and one bullet in a major organ or one shell heading your way will mean oblivion. When I eventually came to my senses it was nearly dusk. Rats had started to come out of their nests to feed on the dead bodies: fresh meat to them. As the dark descended I heard a murmuring. Was it friend or foe? Rifle cocked I crept towards the sound. I peered over the rim of a shell hole with my rifle at the ready. It was a German soldier. My finger was on the trigger, pressure on, ready. "Don't shoot, I'm English," the German pleaded. I hesitated for a second. Was this a trick? Was I being set up to be off my guard and be killed? He was unharmed and was tending to a seriously injured soldier. What could I do, what should I do? Do I kill them both or do I show compassion? I am a human being and nothing in the training manual covers this situation. Could I morally kill a dying man? What would those ladies at the gate say I should do? What if the roles had been reversed? What if it was a dying British soldier being helped by another soldier. What would a German soldier do? Should I have killed the intact soldier and left the injured one to his fate, to the rats? And what about those ladies at the gates? What if it was their husband or son? I had the rifle, so he was my prisoner. The German seemed to have medical experience in the field. I said nothing, just watched. The injured soldier was semi-conscious and to stop him moaning the German had put a rag in his mouth. I could do nothing to help. My gun was trained on the German. 'Don't worry, Tommy,' he said to me. 'I'm out of this shambles. Do what you have to do, I have finished with war.' As night fell, the only light was from a full moon but, as tired as I was, I kept my sight on the two Germans.

'Eventually the injured soldier breathed his last, so it was just the German soldier and myself. Was he my prisoner? I did not think in those terms. As the day broke and the sound of guns seemed many

miles away I asked him his name. He said it was Fritz von Franke. His mother was called Ethel and his father Herbert. I started to interrogate him on his claim to be English and he explained that his mother was English and had met his father while they were both working in the same cotton mill in Oldham. He told me that he spent a lot of time living in Werneth and went on to describe his schooling. I questioned him about Manchester city centre and his answers left me in no doubt that he was telling me the truth. At the start of hostilities his father was ordered to leave England with transport being organised to take them back to Germany. Fritz said that it was a great shock as he considered himself to be English. He was eventually called up by the German army but I believed his story of being brought up in England. Having little food or drink between us, we set off walking in parallel to the battle line where we eventually met up with Allied troops. Fritz realised he was vulnerable in his German uniform and that is when he took the uniform of a dead soldier. On reflection, the decision to walk together in a southerly direction was a mistake and, in hindsight, it was very questionable to put Fritz in that uniform. To take the uniform off a dead soldier leaving him naked and buried in a shallow grave was an act of desperation. I did make a promise to that naked soldier to return his papers to his family and that is something I hope that I will still be able to do at some time in the future.

'*The question that I have asked myself is this: at what stage did this German soldier cease to be "the enemy" and what level of collusion took place? Does the term collusion mean to pass on information to the enemy? If so, then nothing passed between us.*

'*There was no collusion. In effect, Fritz, by wearing the uniform, had changed sides from being German to being an Allied soldier, therefore I am innocent of the third charge but perhaps then the charge of desertion remains? But how can that be if we intended to find action again, as soon as possible? Which is exactly what we did when we linked up with the US Army in the Argonne Forest.'*

The prosecution intervened and looked directly at the judge advocate.

'While we all like to hear about a Boy's Own rescue mission it is totally irrelevant to these proceedings. There are three charges on the table and I have yet to be convinced by Private Fred Mills or his defence lawyer. All this court has heard is drivel more suited to a Christmas pantomime than a general court martial.'

This brought a nod of approval from the judge advocate.

The judge advocate brought the court to attention and told all assembled that both himself and his fellow judges had listened intently to the submission from Private Mills.

'I order that the court leaves the case at that final comment from James Grant KC and re-convenes in two hours' time. I suggest that the defence team spend the intervening time re-considering the story given to this court by Private Mills. I will also allow written statements from individuals or groups who have direct involvement in the outcome of this court martial as long as they do not take too much of the court's time.'

After the break in proceedings the prosecutor stood up, looked round and started his final delivery.

'This is an unusual court martial in that the offences took place nearly four years ago. Four years in which a mother had thought her eldest son to have been killed on the 29 September 1918. That is in itself a callous act: a callous act from a soldier who claims to be compassionate. I could say that this indictment sums up the character of this soldier but let us give him the benefit of the doubt and concentrate on the three contraventions of the military law. Was he a coward and did he desert his post.? Yes or No! Is it no, because he evidently has a fine history as a combatant in several areas, carrying out differing tasks; I think it is safe to assume that this history is of

Fred and not George Mills. Or is it yes, he was a coward and did desert on that day in question? Perhaps the pressure of his time on the front line had taken its toll. He says himself that what was supposed to be "a walk in the park" turned into absolute carnage. The heavy gun fire which was intended to take out the enemy did not take into account the German trenches which were built more solidly, had been dug deeper and had been in use far longer than the British counterparts. The advantage they had was that the defences were built as a permanent feature and the design and structure was such that the Germans had far more protection against shell damage from British artillery bombardment than what had been anticipated. British officers truly thought, as you said, that it would be a walk in the park. But they soon realised that the German defences had not been breached so the gun fire was adjusted to take account of this.

'A military engagement always starts off to a plan, but the fluidity of the battle called for swift and decisive adjustment. This is what happened on the day in question. Private Mills, who claimed to have been involved in many engagements should have been aware of this. Perhaps he just lost his nerve this time.

'If that was the case and he did lose his nerve, causing him to hide from view while his fellow soldiers carried on with the move forward, then he is guilty of desertion, no matter what the criticisms were of the early stages of that battle. Let me reiterate that in spite of the unfortunate circumstances at the beginning of the battle, Private Mills' fellow soldiers carried on forward and took out all the machine gun posts, killed all the snipers and what will go down in history is that they gained between ten and fifteen miles that day and completely took over the impregnable Hindenburg Line. Not a bad day's work, and where was Private Mills? Well, he had been hiding away for an extended period of time, having a nice chat with an enemy soldier about the niceties of Piccadilly Gardens in Manchester. I say he is guilty of desertion, guilty of cowardice and to cap it all, clearly guilty of collusion with the enemy. Being guilty of two offences is serious enough. But colluding with the enemy on top of those two charges puts this court martial in a much higher category than any case that I have been involved in or read about. We are in uncharted waters, there has never been such a serious number of charges in the annals or history of the court martial. I say Private Fred Mills is guilty, guilty, guilty and let the judges determine a suitable punishment. I have checked to see if there is any time limitation on bringing an action for cowardice and desertion and from my reading there is no time limit. If an action happened ten years ago there can still be a case brought against the deserter. The same applies if it had been twenty years ago or even more. With regard to what punishment should be administered. I have no recommendation on what that should be. Thank you.'

The judge advocate turned to the defence lawyer. 'Have you anything to say in reply to that eloquent summing up from the prosecution?'

'I have a lot to say in reply but I do not think that there is enough time in this session to allow me to fully put forward my case and would respectfully ask that we adjourn for today and reconvene for ten am tomorrow.'

The judge advocate turned to the prosecution to seek their approval, which they gave, albeit reluctantly.

Back at Beaurepaire, the defence lawyer suggested that they take thirty minutes to freshen up before meeting in one of the small private lounges to discuss the status of the trial and the next move. Miss Goodwin had organised tea and cakes to lighten the atmosphere and once all parties had re-assembled she commenced with her effort to bring about a more favourable outcome.

'As you are all aware the organisation Mothers of the Fallen have been in attendance during the duration of the trial. The spokesperson for the MOTF is Mrs Cynthia Williams, who as well as being the organiser of that group of ladies, is also very influential. During the previous weekend our paths crossed and we got talking, initially, about general subjects and then we started to talk about the court martial.'

CHAPTER 35:

THE COURT MARTIAL – TOWARDS A CONCLUSION

'I took the opportunity to enlighten Mrs Williams on some specific issues relating to Private Mills and the direction of the court martial. She realised two important facts: firstly, that this case is far removed from the case of those in the Paris nightclub and secondly, that whatever the facts, explanations and circumstances might be, the judge advocate wants the ultimate punishment in order to compensate for the loss of his one and only nephew, the sole heir to his large estate on the south coast. Captain Frederick Charles Shaw was killed on 1 November 1918 by a German officer who had been taken prisoner and appeared grateful to have been put in the safe custody of the British Army. In a split second this German officer diverted the attention of Captain 'Freddie', snatched the officer's pistol that had been trained on him and shot Captain Shaw in the stomach. The judge advocate, who was on duty in the vicinity of the incident, came straight away to the field hospital and stayed with his nephew throughout the agonising and drawn out death that his nephew endured. This is why he is so unsympathetic to any soldier who steps out of line. He is oblivious to any circumstances surrounding a court martial. Whatever is said and done in our case is of no consequence to him. What's more, he will make it clear to the four others judges that the only verdict he will accept is the guilty one. I took it upon myself to arrange an informal meeting between myself, Mrs Williams and Ron Dewhirst where she opened up to us. She said that she had total sympathy with Private Mills and if it would be of any benefit she would draft a statement on behalf of the vast majority of the MOTF. I told her that if she did then I would format the statement to allow those members of the that organisation, in agreement, to sign their name, the name of their fallen loved one plus any other comments. I then suggest it be given to the defence team to present to the court in whatever manner they see fit.'

General Johnson, spoke next. 'I have been in contact with Mr Van de Veldt. Yesterday he had a confidential and unscheduled meeting at the White House in Washington and updated those present with the facts relating to Private Fred Mills. Those present at the meeting were told the details of the court martial and the role of this soldier in the rescue of the encircled US soldiers in the "Argonne Forest". I must also say that I have been uneasy in recent days as I have noticed a build-up of what appears to be British soldiers dressed in civilian clothes in and around Deauville and surrounding resorts.'

The general continued. 'I suspect that if there was a guilty verdict then the British Army have a plan to take Fred Mills back to England, so we will have our own experienced security on hand to ensure that that does not happen, whatever the political consequences. Mr Van de Veldt also received an official communication from the top man in New Zealand. The gist of this was to basically ask if Private Mills could formally prove that the naked soldier is Sergeant Jack Jackson. If he can prove it, then the New Zealand Government will exonerate him from any charge and give him free passage for himself and his good lady to Christchurch NZ where he, and another soldier, will formally unveil the memorial to the fallen. The message from New Zealand is that even if the Sergeant Jackson who took out the machine gun and the Sergeant Jackson who rescued the trapped Americans are different "Jack Jacksons", it is irrelevant. In the annals of NZ history it will become the same man. The details can be kept secret by a few but it will be a secret that dies with them. In fifty years' time people will celebrate ANZAC day and no one will be alive who knew the real facts. That was the message from New Zealand.'

'Whatever the verdict, if the British try to take Fred, by force, into their custody, it will be met with very strong US resistance: resistance that has been given full backing straight from the top. Mr Van de Veldt has a lot of political influence and, trust me, I'm authorised to do whatever is necessary to protect Private Fred Mills. No limits, no restrictions; one way or another Fred will be a free man. Is everybody ok with that? I need everybody to stay calm, to act normally and let my team do their job.'

'There is one final piece to this jigsaw. Through great effort, the VdV organisation has managed to locate Fritz, Jack Jackson or whatever his name was or will be. For reasons known only to Fritz, he and his lady Yvette have changed their names and nationalities. The VdV organisation worked out that the couple would have returned to the Alsace area where his family came from. As we know, this area was French until 1871 then became German and then under the Treaty of Versailles became French again. The German occupants of this vast area of France were relocated within the new German borders as demanded by the Allies through the strict restrictions imposed by the treaty. The VdV organisation worked on the assumption that Fritz and Yvette would become French nationals and as such, they would have needed new identity papers. Through infiltrating the network of people who supply forged documentation and by paying out exceptionally large amounts of money, Fritz and Yvette were traced, and after some persuasion, Fritz has given us a statement detailing his interpretation of the events regarding himself and Fred.

He gave them under the strict condition that his and Yvette's new identities and location are kept secret. I have read the account and in every detail it corresponds with what Fred told the court. I have discussed the value of this statement with the defence team and we feel that it would be counterproductive to bring this statement to the court martial. We could, if necessary, say that we have corroborated evidence; that Fred's story is 100% true and, if necessary, this could be validated by a special committee in the US government.'

The defence lawyer summed up and said that he was happy with the evidence he had at his disposal and that he was confident of convincing at least two of the judges that Private Mills was not guilty of any of the three charges. One of the judges was a personal friend of the judge advocate, so it would be down to one of these other judges to use their own discretion and find the case not proven. That would leave three for and two against Private Mills' freedom. 'The judge to the extreme left is the weakest link in the chain,' he explained, 'so I will bear that in mind in the summing up. If that judge did follow the judge advocate then the British Army would intervene and attempt to arrest Fred and either take him back to England or, in the worst case scenario, take action, without delay, on French soil. I do not think that will happen but we must be prepared. We need to keep our heads clear for tomorrow's session so I have suggested that the bar is closed tonight and the gentleman stood at the far side of the bar is part of the VdV organisation, so be warned. No bar tonight. Goodnight, gentlemen and Miss Goodwin.'

It was a lovely bright morning in Montreuil-sur-Mer and all parties chose to breakfast in their own rooms. Enough was said the previous evening and everyone knew what might happen that day.

The court martial commenced at ten and the defence lawyer stood up to deliver his final statement to the five judges.

'This is an unusual and difficult case for the judges here to deliberate on. It is my duty to bring before this court the facts that clear Private Fred Mills of every one of the three charges laid against him. It is also the duty of the judges to take into account the evidence given by myself and by James Grant KC and make a judgement based on facts, not on bias or any pre-conceived thoughts surrounding this case. This is the fundamental feature of British law. We have seen the word collusion used many times in this court. Any kind of collusion is both evil and unnecessary.

'Each man in a court of law is his own man and any attempt to influence him goes against natural justice. Anyone who stoops so low will themselves be judged and their attempts to pervert the cause of justice will be remembered for all future generations who will, in turn, judge them. I say this to remind us all that the legal system is equal, unbiased and that the ladder of law has no top or bottom.'

The judge advocate intervened. 'Thank you for that lesson on the legal system. Will you present your arguments and enlighten us as to what makes you so sure that these three charges do not apply to Private Fred Mills?'

The defence lawyer nodded. 'I am very sure of the innocence of Private Fred Mills and I will answer the three cases laid against him. The actual, historical events of what happened on the day Fred Mills is accused of cowardice and desertion has already been explained to you in great detail. It has been made very clear to the court what the conditions were on that day: there was a great deal of confusion in an atmosphere of complete chaos and this has been backed up, confirmed and corroborated by the retired Major George Haig, who was involved in the heat of the battle. The whole day was thrown into confusion. This is a fact that has been well established. Anyone who has been involved at the sharp end of a charge on enemy lines will fully understand that there is never a simple and predictable outcome. The attack was organised on a very broad front and some advancements made greater inroads than others. All of you who sit here and will later make a final judgement on this man, all of you have seen major actions. All of you understand the battlefield and have first-hand knowledge of how it can be. You know that the role of senior officers is to manage actions, order changes and consolidate gains in response to circumstances. What a senior officer cannot do is get physically involved in a thrust forward. That role is the duty of junior officers: these officers tend to lead from the front and unfortunately those junior officers became thin on the ground on the day in question as they accounted for a disproportionate number of the casualties. This is evidenced in the situation of Captain Stephen, who, having been seriously injured, was briefly aided by Private Mills, aid that the prosecution has deemed "hiding" instead of moving forward. This court martial has heard enough evidence regarding the events of the 29 September: enough to dismiss the charge of cowardice and desertion on the day in question. You question where Private Fred Mills was between the mid/late morning of that day and the early evening just before dusk when he encountered the German, Fritz. Without having actual experience of the conditions on a major thrust into enemy lines, I admit that in twenty-five plus years as an officer I have never encountered any situation remotely comparable to what Private Mills and thousands of other soldiers had to endure. But I have had hands-on experience of the condition known as shell shock, in its many forms. I propose that Private Mills became disorientated and found the direction of the battle difficult to judge.

'In a state of confusion, he could easily have drifted into the German sector, which certainly seems to be the case when he found himself at a shell hole with two Germans inside. We will never know for sure, so we cannot make definite judgements due to the lack of known facts. So let us give due respect to a front-line soldier and dismiss these two charges.

'Taking the third charge of collusion with the enemy, I fail to understand where such collusion occurred. The German, Fritz, was unarmed and gave himself up to Private Mills willingly. There was no collusion, no force from Private Mills. The German soldier's statement indicates that he had had enough and made that very clear to Private Mills. Don't forget that the soldiers truly believed that as a result of their actions the war would be over within a few days. Their mindset was such that if they could just survive another two days, then they could well be going home and the carnage would end. That was the honest belief of soldiers fighting to take the German defence line. The German soldier, Fritz, deserted his line. That was the only "desertion" that day.

'Collusion, no! Capture of a prisoner of war, yes.

'Under the Geneva Convention, it is forbidden to kill or to injure an enemy who surrenders or is 'hors de combat'. I am certain that you, the judges, are fully aware of the responsibilities of any soldier who captures one of the enemy and how that soldier must conduct himself if an enemy soldier removes himself from battle. Under the strict terms of the Geneva Convention, Private Mills is in no way guilty of collusion with the enemy. In fact, he was doing his duty.

'Being in a battle situation is the most frightening circumstance that one could ever imagine. Your life is hanging by a thread and in these conditions you do what you can to preserve both the lives of your fellow soldiers and ultimately your own. I now bring to your attention an historical case to make a comparison. A junior officer fighting in the Boer War found himself alone and isolated. Was this junior officer correct to hide under an upturned wagon for the best part of a day until relief came and the enemy was defeated? Was that cowardice? Was that desertion? I say no. This officer survived a terrible event but serves the British Army to this day. His senior officer at that time was, in fact, his uncle, not that it had any influence. There was no court martial, just common sense being applied by the senior officer, uncle or not.'

The judge advocate visibly paled and winced when he heard this account.

'I am permitted to bring before the judges statements which may help in their deliberations.

The first to consider is a statement from the Mothers of the Fallen, a vocal group of mothers, wives and sisters of those soldiers who made the ultimate sacrifice while serving king and country. I will read out the statement summary but will hand over a copy of the statement for the judges to read in full:

'"We, Mothers of the Fallen, are a group of women who have lost loved ones during the recent conflict. We were brought together in response to appalling revelations in a Paris nightclub just after the Armistice was signed. Soldiers in Paris were boasting about how they had saved their own skin with no regard or concern for their fellow soldiers. This caused great anger in all the mothers, wives and sisters of those who had fought bravely to the bitter end. We called for the soldiers in Paris to stand trial, to be court martialled; we made it very clear that, if found guilty, those soldiers should be made to suffer the ultimate sacrifice and face the firing squad. At the outset we considered that the court martial of Private Fred Mills was a case in the same ilk.

'"Having kept abreast of each day's proceedings and making it our business to discover the facts for ourselves, we find that Private Fred Mills acted in an honourable manner. He went on to carry out one of the most daring rescue attempts in the annals of warfare. The names undersigned represent nearly 90 per cent of our members. Please consider this statement from a dedicated group of women who have suffered greatly because of the war. Thank you, Mrs Cynthia Williams, wife of Lieutenant Colonel T J Williams (fallen)."'

General Johnston then took to the floor.

'Judges, I am General Paul Johnston of the US Army. I have been working with Mr Ron Dewhirst and Miss Gill Goodwin, who are both senior executives of the VdV organisation, a global company based in New York under the ownership of Mr Joseph Van de Veldt, a billionaire business man. Mr Van de Veldt's interest in Private Fred Mills stems from the soldier's role in rescuing American soldiers held captive under appalling conditions in the Argonne Forest. While I fully appreciate that the rescue attempt has no relevance to the court martial, it still must be taken into consideration as it demonstrates the bravery, commitment and resilience of both Private Mills and his colleague. This soldier stands before you, an example of ultimate bravery, a bravery matched by very few human beings in the whole history of conflict.' General Johnston paused to look the judge advocate in the eye. 'He didn't hide under an upturned wagon until rescue came; he did what he had to do without any consideration of the risks to himself. Mr Van de Veldt has already offered a large sum of money to help set up Fred and his lady Else in a business venture whenever, wherever and in whatever they wish. Through the resources of the VdV organisation we have been able to clarify the identity of the naked soldier and can now reassure the people of New Zealand and Canterbury, in particular, that Private Fred Mills has taken great care of the personal effects of Sergeant Jack Jackson and will return them to the family as soon as he is able. Private Mills has already heard that the frontal attack on the machine gun post carried out by Sergeant Jack Jackson also involved another brave soldier: Lance Corporal George Mills, close cousin of Fred. God willing, they will by re-united at the commemoration of the memorial to the fallen with the remains of Sergeant Jack Jackson re-interned under the memorial itself. I am quite sure that Fred will be amazed at this news concerning his cousin and I will happily fill him in with all the details at the end of this court martial.'

The general took a sip of water and continued.

'Perhaps I am jumping the gun talking about the future of Private Mills, as his future lies in the hands of these learned officers: the judges seated here before us. I have yet to receive a document which may prove most influential in this case. I am still waiting for it to arrive; it looks like the delay is caused by time differences and some technical issues in the area of the court.'

General Johnson finished by thanking the judges for allowing his statements to be read out and expressed his confidence, that in the judge's ensuing deliberations, Private Fred Mills would be cleared of all charges against him.

CHAPTER 36:
THE COURT MARTIAL – THE VERDICT

The judge advocate turned to his fellow judges and suggested a two-hour break in proceedings to enable them to discuss the charges and to have some late lunch. Throughout the duration of the court martial, an arrangement had been made that lunch, for the five judges, would be prepared by the head chef of the Normandie Hotel in Deauville. As it was to be the final lunch, the head chef came to the court, prepared the meal and presented it to the judges.

They ate a very fine haunch of venison that the chef had prepared preceded by a plate of fine oysters, finished off with a crepe. The wine to complement the venison was a very fine 1917 Chateau La Tour Grand Margaux from Bordeaux. The judge advocate proposed a toast to his fellow judges and suggested that they concentrate on the food and wine while discussing their favourites for the following weeks racing at Longchamp and Chantilly.

As a result, the proposed two-hour recess passed quickly and the outcome of the court martial had yet to be discussed.

'Gentlemen,' the judge advocate began, 'let us now attend to the verdict. I take it that we are unanimous in believing that all three charges against Private Mills have been proven and that we can bring this court martial to an end as soon as possible.'

Judges A and B confirmed that all three charges should stand, but judges C and D expressed doubts both factually and morally.

'Am I hearing correctly? You have heard the eloquent presentation by James Grant KC of the Crown's case against this private and yet you are hesitating on doing what you were brought here to do: to protect the integrity of the British Army! Justice must be meted out strongly for penalty and repentance. If we shirk our responsibilities there will be anarchy in the ranks. I suggest that both of you pull yourselves together and reconsider so we can get this business over and done with.

'I recommend that you both withdraw to one of the ante-rooms for thirty minutes to reconsider your verdict. When you have come to your senses, we will go back into the court and finish off our job. It will be a poor show if four senior British officers, acting as judges, cannot all agree on a unanimous verdict so putting the final responsibility on myself as the judge advocate. If you let me and your country down, I will personally see to it that life is made just a little bit more difficult for the both of you and that is not a threat, it is a promise. So, thirty minutes, no longer. I have a dinner appointment at the Chateau Montpinchon this evening and I have not the slightest intention of being late, so I strongly suggest that you sort yourselves out.'

The two opposing judges held their discussions, both concerned about the consequences of going against the judge advocate. Their lifestyles were financed by more than adequate pensions in the comfortable suburbs of London, so why, they considered, should they 'rock the boat'? As a result, they decided to forget their moral objections, forget their doubts on the strength of the prosecution case and just agree with the other judges, but also hoped that Private Mills would be dealt with in a reasonable manner without going for the firing squad.

Just short of the thirty minutes they re-joined the judge advocate and the other two judges. The former welcomed them back. 'I assume that you have come to your senses and we can give the court our judgement.'

The five judges took their seats and asked both the defence and the prosecution legal team to stand while the judge advocate gave his summing up.

'I have sat in judgement on many court martials during the last ten years and never have I come across a more open-and-close case as the one put before us over the past weeks. Here we have a so-called hero who may well have carried out deeds to help the US Army. An army whose arrival into the fray was significantly late. It is the opinion of several senior members of the British Army that this late arrival, rather than shorten the duration of the war, actually set a challenge to the German people to continue the fight and teach the naïve American forces a lesson. The facts, as told to me, are that without US involvement the war would have ended in late 1917 with the Allies giving the Germans an easy exit without the harsh punishments contained in the Treaty of Versailles. Many senior officers fear that the harshness of the Treaty will have serious repercussions in years to come.

'Here we have before us a soldier who made no attempt to contact his family, either directly or indirectly, so as to reassure them that he had survived the attack on the 29 September and, indeed, that he had survived the rest of the war.

'His defence lawyer relied on the nephew of Lord Haig, who gave details of a fleeting glance as sufficient evidence that Private Mills was no coward. Would a coward have lost five or six hours of the 29th? Would he have got lost in a successful push against formidable well-structured defences? When all his fellow soldiers pushed forward Private Mills, allegedly suffering from some unrecognised illness they call 'shell shock', was wandering away from the fight, supposedly disorientated. The excuse of shell shock is manna from heaven for all the shirkers and skivers in the British Army. Have no doubt: Private Mills was a coward on the 29 September and as such he has tarnished his record for fine soldiering in previous encounters. He let himself down!

'So that leaves the third charge of collusion.

'The defence has made great play of the responsibilities of soldiers under the Geneva Convention and Private Mills' lack of knowledge and training to cover the situation he was in. In war, no two situations are the same and to have a proper understanding of the Geneva Convention is far beyond the capabilities of a rank and file solider. It was his duty to use his judgement in the circumstances he was in. The judgement he made, considering his level of soldiering, was a poor one. That is why we have officers. It is the officers who make the important decisions and high-level judgements. Officers who are trained to lead and who come from good families: families that have history, families that have standards, families who have by nature good judgement. Private Mills is not blessed with such high standards. That is why he has been found guilty of collusion and that is all that needs to be said on the matter.

'I find the accused Private Fred Mills, serial number 30103 of the Duke of Cornwall's Light Infantry guilty on all three counts of cowardice, desertion and treason. Before I pass the sentence I will grant the Defence Lawyer Mr Frederick Watson-Hill a very brief moment to respond to the verdict.'

The defence lawyer did not seem surprised at the verdict and stood before the judges calm and unconcerned. 'I did hope that at least two of the judges might have had the strength of character to think for themselves. But, unfortunately, that does not seem to be the case. I surmise, therefore, that if there had been an upturned wagon, then Private Mills could have availed himself of its shelter and nothing would have been said about it.'

CHAPTER 37:
THE GREAT ESCAPE

The defence lawyer surveyed the room. 'General Johnson did say earlier that he was waiting for an important document to arrive and I can confirm that it has arrived and that the general has passed it to me. I now have this final piece of information in my possession and I will read the contents.'

The judge advocate looked at his pocket watch. 'Get on with it, let us get these proceedings concluded.'

The defence lawyer cleared his throat and read the document.

'It is from the secretary of state of the Government of the United States of America and it is dated with yesterday's date.

'"I am proud to confirm that Fred Mills, private of the Duke of Cornwall's Light Infantry, serial number 30103, as of today, has been granted full USA citizenship and is, subsequently, covered by the jurisdiction and protection of the US government. He is instructed that, together with his lady, Else, they will leave that place, accompanied by four US special soldiers who will take them to a waiting vehicle. From there they will be transported to the port of Le Havre where Fred will be honoured with recognition of the supreme act of bravery carried out in the Argonne Forest in October 1918. They will be taken on board the US Frigate *State of Rhode Island* and at the limit of international waters, formalities will commence.

'"They are to be accompanied by US Special Forces to ensure

their safe passage to America."

'It is signed and dated as follows: F Wilson Brown. Witnessed by and dated: President Woodrow Wilson.'

The prosecutor, James Grant KC, looked towards the judge advocate for guidance but got no response.

The defence lawyer stood to announce just one more item. 'It was pointed out earlier by the learned prosecution that there is, in fact, no time limit to bring cases of cowardice and desertion to justice. I believe that the time limit of twenty years was even mentioned as still being irrelevant in cases of desertion and cowardice. I wish the judges to bear that in mind as I bring to their attention the case of Charles Shaw, who was involved in the attack on Mafeking during what has become named as the Second Boer War.'

The defence lawyer looked at the judge advocate. 'We have before us the junior officer from that incident. Charles Shaw, the judge advocate. The same person who presides over this court martial having the ultimate sanction of life or death over this brave solider, who fought bravely for his king and country and did not hide under an upturned wagon to avoid doing his duty.'

'I have in my possession a statement signed by the captain involved in the incident and the company sergeant major in charge of carrying out the orders of that day. This statement names a junior officer who deliberately hid under an upturned wagon instead of leading a squad of infantry to take a Boer-held position. The lack of direction, which should have come from this officer, resulted in the savage deaths of all twenty soldiers under his command.

'The officer was found the next day when a strong force of British soldiers regained the position. On hearing familiar voices the junior officer came out of his hiding place and claimed to have fought until he was the last man standing. That might have been plausible if not for the dribble of excreta running down his legs. He had shit himself rather than fight. Although the event was reported no action was taken and it was swept under the carpet. But, given there is no time limit set on prosecuting deserters, we can now set the wheels in motion to see if any contravention of the military act occurred during this incident.'

While all attention was focused on the judge advocate's reaction to the potential charge made by Watson-Hill, the rest of his defence team left the building to return back to their hotels, rewarding themselves with a small celebratory drink.

Fred and Else followed Miss Goodwin. They sat alongside four soldiers in a US Army vehicle and were soon on their way to Le Havre. During the drive, Miss Goodwin explained to Fred and Else that the first part of the journey was a decoy. In a few minutes they would stop and Fred and Else would be transferred to a common unmarked vehicle to be taken to Boulogne where Mr Van de Veldt would be waiting to welcome them on board his private yacht. Miss Goodwin explained that to complete the deception two people of Else and Fred's sizes, dressed in a similar manner would be placed in the original vehicle and taken on a 'wild goose chase' to Le Havre. The VdV yacht with Fred and Else aboard was to sail from Boulogne to San Sebastian in Spain where they would stay in the Hotel Maria Christina under the name of Mr and Mrs Dewhirst for five nights while the VdV organisation presented various options to Fred and Else. For example, should they wish to be married, then San Sebastian was a truly beautiful setting and a wedding could be arranged.

Back in the confusion and uncertainty of the court martial, James Grant KC took charge of the situation, contacted the British high commissioner in Paris and spoke to his assistant, telling him of the events that had taken place at the end of the court martial. The assistant interrupted his boss, who immediately contacted the

US embassy himself, requesting to speak to the senior officer in charge. After discussions at the highest level, it transpired that the US government had no knowledge regarding the offer of citizenship to Fred Mills. An urgent telegram was sent to the White House, who confirmed that they had no knowledge of the offer of citizenship. After some internal debate in the seat of US government it transpired that no physical copy of the document was handed over, it was only read as a draft prepared by Mr Ron Dewhirst.

The British high commissioner suggested that the French or British Navy should stop the frigate *State of Rhode Island* but phone calls down the lines of authority soon established that there was no such vessel in the US navy or any that sounded even vaguely familiar.

The dialogue between senior personnel in Britain and the US took the better part of three days and only came to an end via a telegram from the US president to the British prime minister, tactfully suggesting that the British government had been duped.

'I'm sorry for what has happened and that your people fell for it, but it can be quite simple to carry out such subversive actions if documents are readily accepted and no one thinks to check out the facts.' When the circumstances were aired in congress the ensuing laughter nearly brought the roof down. While the news of the end of the court martial was kept out of the British news, the headlines on the front page of the New York Times read 'Brits conned, but it's easily done!'

CHAPTER 38:

CONCLUSION

During the all too brief stay in San Sebastian, Fred and Else made two decisions. Firstly, they would get married, which they did in the Basilica de Santa Maria in San Sebastian. Secondly, they would take up an offer from Mr Van de Veldt to purchase a sheep farm on New Zealand's South Island, which they discovered would neighbour the dairy farm that was to be purchased for his cousin George, his wife and their children. Both farms were up and running with quality management in place, but, if there were ever any issues the VdV organisation would be on hand to help and this promise would be written in the VdV statute books.

The following twelve months were taken up sorting out Else's personal finances and organising some quality time for Fred and George to spend with their families. Fred spent a week at the Imperial Hotel in Blackpool with his mother, although he did have to be booked in under an assumed name. Fred's father chose to stay in Chadderton as he had commitments to play 'brag' and dominoes at the Five O'clock Club in the Hunt Lane Tavern where he was a popular host at the corner table near the window. His winnings on a five-fold bet had left him with plenty of loose change to cover the cost of the beer for his gang. He'd had a good week receiving the news that his son, Fred, had turned up in New Zealand after having suffered amnesia from a shell that had exploded a few yards from him causing his Fred to suffer from something called shell shock.

The charge against Charles 'Shitty' Shaw became public news, causing this stalwart of the British Army to become a quivering wreck. After a nervous breakdown, the Crown decided that Charles Shaw was not fit to be subjected to a court martial. By agreement with his family, his army record was expunged and after a short illness he quietly passed away quietly at a nursing home in Sussex.

The re-assessment of all court martial cases he had participated in resulted in half of his judgements being reversed and, where applicable, some measure of compensation offered. But no amount of compensation could bring back the poor lads who had been shot at dawn.

The case against Private Fred Mills was erased from the records with Fred exonerated from any wrongdoing. Both Fred and George rejected the offers of acknowledgement from the British government, including a suggestion that their gallantry be rewarded with the highest possible recognition.

The journey from Northern Spain to New Zealand took four months and during that time the memorial to the fallen was completed to a modified design. The sculptor had convinced the committee that the memorial would be more dramatic with a design highlighting the forward action of the sergeant with another of his team slightly behind him. It was decided that the face of the second soldier should not be identified with any of the other five members of the attack.

The body of Sergeant Jack Jackson was exhumed and transferred to Canterbury in readiness for his ceremonial internment at the foot of the memorial. It had been arranged that Private Fred Mills would hand over the personal papers to Sergeant Jackson's widow in a private ceremony, the papers being contained in a silver box, designed and financed by the VdV organisation and certified by a Swiss specialist in historical and personal documents.

The whole of Canterbury attended the opening of the memorial and the interment of Sergeant Jackson. The two actions of both Jack Jackson(s) were read out by the prime minister of New Zealand and delivered in such a way as to suggest that the attack on the gun shelter and the rescue of the US soldiers were carried out by the one man.

To compensate for their loss, the VdV organisation arranged a reward for Sergeant Jackson's family and granted his widow an annual pension, paid weekly, equivalent to ten times the income of Jack Jackson prior to him joining the NZ army.

Both Fred and George Mills were enthusiastically welcomed and after staying a few days in Christchurch they were transported to their new homes. They were eager to see where they would be spending their lives in the future. As the first of the farm houses came into view, gasps of excitement could be heard from both wives.

There before them stood a beautiful building in a beautiful setting.

Fred and Else walked up the drive to their home and were surprised to see all the staff and workers lined up, clapping them into their new residence. After all the years of adversity Fred was not embarrassed to shed a tear or two because he and Else had just walked into dreamland, and thanks to Mr Van de Veldt they should live very happy ever after.

THE END

DEDICATION

The book is dedicated to the heroes from the Cotton Mills of Oldham who formed the Oldham Pals Brigade and who fought courageously against German aggressors.

In particular, I wish to preserve the memory of my uncle, Fred Mills who fought with the Duke of Cornwall's Light Infantry (30103) and was killed in action on the 29 September 1918 during the Battle for the Hindenburg Line, which was the first line of the German defensive system. The Allies were confident that once this line of resistance fell then it would only be a matter of days before the Germans surrendered.

The German army continued for another six weeks before the war finally ended on the 11 November 1918.

Fred, along with other members of the DCLI, was 'killed in action' during the advancement on the village of La Vacquerie. The officer in charge of the DCLI, Captain Stephen Girling, lost his life that day and his body is interred in the Fifteen Ravine British War Cemetery a short distance from the village that was freed from German hands on that day. Fred and several other members of the DCLI are commemorated in this cemetery, but, as is the case for the majority of deaths on the battlefield, there is no name to put to the remains, only the inscription:

'Here lies a soldier whose name is known only to God.'

Fred's name is remembered on a panel of the Vis-en-Artois Cemetery located on the main road between Arras and Cambrai. It is significant that the vast majority of those remembered in this way have no grave. Only a minority of soldiers have a body with a name. This reflects the carnage upon carnage that these soldiers suffered just over one hundred years ago fighting for this war to end all wars. But it didn't 'end all wars' and just twenty-one years later the next generation of soldiers had to suffer the same ordeal.

My father, Harold, told me that Fred had not been killed, but had carried on fighting with his friends from New Zealand and had, he believed, moved to the other side of the world to start a new life. This was possibly a story to pacify his mother, Mary Anne, who had lost her eldest son.

Although Fred's name is remembered on the Vis-en-Artois memorial in France he is not remembered on the war memorial in his home town of Chadderton. I have the standard communication from the War Office that informs the family upon the death of a soldier and have noticed that this should have been returned with Fred's details to the War Office. It's a bit late now to sort that out.

Or is it?

It is difficult to fully comprehend the situation that these young men, from both sides, found themselves in. They would not really understand the meaning of war, not until they found themselves in a life or death situation.

The History of The Duke of Cornwall's Light Infantry 1914–1919 by Everard Wyrall gives an in-depth account of the actions of the Cornwall's during the Great War.
On the 29th the Fourth Army at 5:50 am launched the main attack.

The heavy and continuous bombardment, which had begun on the morning of the 27th, had continued for two days without intermission. This bombardment was awe-inspiring and terrible, causing the enemy's garrison to take refuge in their deep tunnels and dug-outs, cutting off his ammunition and ration-carrying and generally reducing his troops to a state bordering on terror.

The 1st DCLA, moved to their assembly positions at 1:30 am on the 29th. The attack was to begin at 3:30 am.

The Cornwall's had only just reached their assembly trenches when the barrage opened up and they had at once to advance. The object was the La Vacquerie Road.

It soon became evident that the barrage was moving too fast for the troops who, having to go forward over broken ground cut up by trenches, also wire and other obstacles, found it impossible to keep pace with it. Moreover, the advance was uphill. The consequence was that the barrage got too far ahead, giving the enemy an opportunity of meeting the attack with heavy machine gun fire. By 12:30 pm the Cornwall's had pushed forward and made contact with New Zealand companies and pushed forward towards La Vacquerie. Over 320 prisoners and about 60 machine guns were taken, of which 100 prisoners and 30 machine guns had been captured by the Cornwall's.

The Cornwall's suffered seventy-five casualties from the ranks (assuming Fred Mills was amongst them) and two officers, one being Lieut. Stephen Girling, (Fred's officer).

The brigade dairy described the day's operation:

Taking into consideration the short notice given of the pending attack and the march of 3 km in darkness to positions of assembly, and the fact that they had barely reached positions when they had to attack, ***The strength, fortitude and gallantry with which these attacks were pressed home by the men, cannot be too highly commended.***

A passage from Remarque's book 'All Quiet on the Western Front' illustrates this from the German viewpoint.

Continuous fire, defensive fire, curtain fire, trench mortars, gas, tanks, machine-guns, hand-grenades – words, words, but they embrace all the horrors of the world.

Our faces are encrusted in dirt, our thoughts are a shambles, we are dead tired; when the attack comes, a lot of our men have to be punched hard so that they wake up and go along; our eyes are red and swollen, our hands are ripped, our knees are bleeding and our elbows raw.

Is it weeks that pass – or months – or years? It is only days. We watch how time disappears before our eyes in ashen faces of the dying, we shovel food into ourselves, we run, we throw, we shoot, we kill, we hurl ourselves down, we are weak and dulled, the only thing that keeps us going is that there are even weaker, even more dulled, even more helpless men than us who look at us wide eyed, and take us for gods who can sometimes out run death himself.

We see men go on living with the top of their skulls missing; we see soldiers go on running when both their feet have been shot away – they stumble on their splintering stumps to the nest shell hole. One lance-corporal crawls for a full half mile on his hands, dragging his legs behind him, with both knees shattered. Another man makes it to a dressing station with his guts spilling out over his hands as he holds them in. We see soldiers with their mouths missing, and their lower jaws missing, with their faces missing; we find someone who has gripped his main artery in his arm between his teeth for two hours so that he doesn't bleed to death.

The sun goes down, night falls, the shells whistle, life comes to an end.

THE END – BUT IT WASN'T